Blue Ocean

M.L. Hendry

To Shane

ISBN: 978-1-7640382-3-2

Cover art created by Matthew Hendry

Shadow and Life Runes designed by Travis Ibbotson

Weather Runes designed by Angela Hendry

***

First Edition

The Shadow Runes

 Shade

 Beam

 Wave

 Height

 Kinetic

The Life Runes

 Protect

 Call

 Grow

 Devine

 See

The Weather Runes

 Torrent

 Rumble

 Flame

 Breeze

 Bolt

Chapter One

A sharp cry escaped Drew's lips as the rune's vision faded and the world snapped back into focus. In his hand was a rune – the *See* rune – granting him glimpses of possible futures. Duchess Wilder had warned him time and again not to put too much stock in what it showed. The visions were always vague: seas, conflict, darkness. And yet, he could not help himself. Even now, on vacation.

His quest to bring peace to Harleland was complete. A year had passed since King Lekt and Duke – now *Grand* Duke – Shârvous of the Crownlands ended the long and brutal war. Harleland had formally recognised the Crownlands as a Sovereign Grand Dutchy, independent from Boron Nigh.

Yet not all was settled. Though the Herk battalions had withdrawn from the Greenarch Plain, the Crownlands maintained control over Canterbury, its Dutchy capital. Friction lingered in Boron Nigh's halls of power, but King Lekt and Chief Naz of the New Protectors had accepted that some concessions were necessary for peace.

The runes were ten magical artefacts Drew carried in his coat pocket. They had aided him many times, but he could not stop relying on them, even in peace. The Shadow Runes – gifted by the late King Lakton – had once filled his mind with whispers of glory, not quite words but impressions he could not ignore. But since finding the Life Runes, those whispers had quieted, replaced by a gentler voice offering reassurance. Like an angel and a devil on his shoulders, the two kinds of runes had once battled for his attention. Now, the darkness was mostly gone.

"Drew!" called Duchess Wilder.

The Lady of Wilder Forest approached, her expression sharp with irritation.

"How many times must I say – don't trust what the *See* rune shows you!" Her voice softened. "It's only a guide."

"I like looking into the future," Drew admitted with a shrug. "It makes me feel important. Like a wise man helping guide his kingdom."

Wilder chuckled. "You're definitely wise, Drew. But you're not old enough to be a true wise man. They're all dull and grey-haired."

"I hope I'm not that boring yet!"

"Of course we don't think that!" said a new voice. General Sylvia, head of Wilder Forest's Warriors, approached with a smirk. "At least I don't think we do," she added playfully.

Wilder smiled.

Drew laughed. "I've still got a while before any grey hairs appear."

He enjoyed their company, though frustration tugged at him. The *See* rune had shown nothing clear – just fog and the echoes of distant battles. It was as if the mist hid something not yet ready to reveal itself. From the top level of Fortuna's ancient tree temple, the place Duchess Wilder made her home, Drew could gaze out over the forest canopy. The fresh scent of the wild and the songs of birds filled the air. On clear days, one could just make out Boron Nigh and the Dirtgula Mountains. Today, clouds hid the capital.

In a few days, King Lekt would host a celebration for the one-year anniversary of the truce. Drew would attend. Wilder had declined the invitation, her relationship with Lekt strained since the invasion of Fortuna. When Lekt disobeyed Wilder's orders and tortured prisoners, it shattered any chance of reconciliation. Sylvia had tried to resign afterward, but Wilder refused, insisting she stay as General.

Drew looked forward to reuniting with his friends – Geetie, Josh, Octavia and Tenebrae. Then there was Naz. Now Chief of the New Protectors, he had risen to his new post during the rebellion against the Uprising movement, a coup that had installed Count Balnather as a false king. Balnather and the other Inquisitors of the movement had met grim ends. Since Lekt's return, no one had dared challenge his rule. Though peace with the Crownlands remained uneasy, it was the most stability Harleland had known in Drew's lifetime.

He breathed in deeply, took one last look at the forest view, and returned inside.

***

Over breakfast, Wilder praised the work Drew, Naz, and the others had done. Wilder Forest was thriving, and Drew was to leave for Boron Nigh that afternoon.

"Send my regards to Chief Naz," said Wilder, before biting into her tofu.

"Why won't you come?" Drew asked, trying to read her striking, hazel-green eyes. "This could be a chance to mend things with King Lekt."

She held his gaze for a long moment, then looked away. "It's not my place. You're the hero, not me. And Lekt… what happened was his choice. I can't forgive it."

"I'd like you to come. At least try. There's room on my horse for both of us."

"I'm sorry, Drew. I can't."

He nodded, disappointed. He would miss her.

After breakfast, Drew wandered alone through Fortuna's gardens, reflecting on the past year. Prince Lekt had gone missing, and Count Balnather sent Drew to find and arrest him. But after a skirmish in the West Bay of Boron Nigh, Drew and Josh became fugitives. A vision had led them to Wilder Forest, meeting back up with Tenebrae along the way, and eventually finding the missing prince. He remembered the terror of the Herk invasion, but also the awe of planting the Seed of Lazarka, which sprouted the legendary Green Tree, and gifted them the Life Runes.

Returning to Boron Nigh, Drew and his companions joined the Revolt that reclaimed the city. Then came the Crownland invasion. A major Herk battalion, led by Shârvous himself, descended on the city during the chaos. Drew used the Life Runes for the first time to shield Boron Nigh with a protective barrier.

He sighed as he remembered the passing of King Lakton. However, it was his son Lekt who, in his first moments as King, met with Shârvous to negotiate peace. Before it was signed, Shârvous executed Count Balnather as he attempted to flee.

Poetic, Drew thought. The supposed villain silencing the schemer. But was Shârvous still a villain? He had honoured the truce for twelve months. Ambassadors reported nothing but courtesy from his court at the Black Fortress of Crown's Crossing.

Drew was not sure. But as he mounted his horse to leave for Boron Nigh, he felt deeply grateful for a year without war.

"Good luck, Drew," Wilder said as she approached to bid farewell.

"Thank you, Duchess," he replied. "I hope I can return soon."

"You'll always be welcome."

"Enjoy the party!" Sylvia called.

Drew waved, then turned toward the trees. The Duchess and her General watched silently, as if each lost in thought, as he disappeared into the forest.

Chapter Two

Once upon a time, the Kingdom of Xudm was the envy of all the lands in the south of Nearth – a land of trade, craftsmanship, and light. But that was before the Belrench came. Fifty years ago, King Mathieu seized Xudm by force. Now his son, King Benjamin the Great, continued the occupation with an iron grip.

For Pho, though, those tales felt distant and impossible. King Ben was a name whispered with fear – too powerful to ever challenge. She lay awake, staring at the ceiling, wondering once more what life had been like before the occupation. Life in Belrench-occupied Xudm was hard. People like her were treated differently to those from Belrance itself, all of them much lighter skinned and dressed in high quality garments and armour. For example, her father wore the same tatty clothes day in and day out, and his tanned skin was often the subject of many jokes from the Belrench officers who watched over her village.

Pho rolled over onto her left side. She could not seem to get comfortable tonight. That was probably because tomorrow she was meant to meet with a man named Commander Luis Occitanie, whom her parents had decided she should marry. Her father, sick of being treated as lower class compared to the Belrench, had formulated the plan. If his daughter were to marry a Belrench officer – one who was in line to become the next Lord of Xudm, no less – then the family would achieve some sort of standing in Belrench society. He had often talked about it with both Pho and her mother. But one thing that her father had failed to consider was Pho's own opinions. She had no desire to wed with any Belrench man, let alone Commander Luis. He was loud, brutish and slimy. He often made rude and quite frankly lecherous comments towards both Pho and most of the other Xudist women who lived in the village of Phārā.

Pho rolled over onto her right side. She puffed in frustration. Sleep would not come tonight. Angrily, she rose from her bed and went over to the window. Her room was not big, yet when she was younger, she shared it with her two siblings, both of whom had married and moved out long ago. Her sister had married a Xudist man and they moved to the neighbouring village of Maṭṭā, while her brother had married a woman from the Augustan Empire and moved far over the sea to be with her. Now she had the room to herself.

It was a clear night, and from her window she could make out the beach. It was a long beach, stretching for miles from the small port in her home village all the way to the north-eastern tip of Xudm. Cliffs loomed over the beach for most of the way, and small caves were often hidden in the rock face. Pho loved the beach, and one of the few freedoms she seemed to have was collecting clams and shells from the shore.

She smiled as she remembered her shell collection. Pho moved away from the window and approached a chest on the far side of her room. Opening it, she looked at the large collection of shells she had found over the years. She wondered what these shells' stories were. Where had they come from? Where had they been? Perhaps they had come from far over the sea. Pho returned to her bed and lay down. She could hear the waves of the Sea of Many Currents crashing against the shore away in the distance. What lay over the sea? She closed her eyes and imagined what it would be like to cross the mighty blue ocean that she had spent her entire life living next to. This was enough to finally send Pho to sleep.

***

"You need to put in much more effort than that if you're going to attract Luis' attention!"

Pho's father was lecturing her about her choice of clothing for her 'meeting' with Commander Luis. They were to meet up in the village square, with Luis supposedly meant to take Pho for a picnic at the beach near Phārā.

"Oh I'm sure she looks fine, Chip!" cried her mother, looking at the man in annoyance.

"It's too casual, Thu!" Chip responded. "How is she going to stand out from the other girls? You know how important it is to our family that Luis marries Pho!"

Pho dropped her head and remained silent. Once more, her father seemed to ignore her feelings. She knew better than to say something to him. He would just accuse her of being against the family's interests. Or something like that. She looked at her attire. To be perfectly honest, she had purposely dressed as plainly as possible in the hopes that Commander Luis would see her as unattractive. Perhaps he would lose interest and she would no longer have to go through with potentially marrying him.

"Oh there's no time to change now!" called Chip in frustration. "Come, come, you'd better get to the village square. Luis will be waiting for you!"

Pho stared at the ground, her shoulders slumped in defeat. Her father ignored her sullen posture, but her mother offered her a reassuring smile. As they stepped out of the house and began the short walk to the village square, her mother fell into step beside her.

"I know you have reservations about Luis," Thu said gently, her voice low but steady. "But this is for the greater good. Our family will be secure, and Luis can give you a life of comfort and wealth. They say the homes in Belrance are the pinnacle of luxury."

Thu's tone lacked conviction. Pho wondered if her mother believed it – or just needed to. For a fleeting moment, she almost allowed herself to agree. The thought of silk cushions and endless feasts shimmered before her. But something inside her wavered. Could she truly trade her freedom for a gilded cage?

The village square soon came into view, bustling with activity. By the lion statue at the center, Commander Luis waited, leaning casually against the carved stone. His immaculate uniform gleamed in the sunlight.

"Chip!" Luis called out warmly as they approached. "It's good to see you again, my friend."

"And you," her father replied, his tone overly jovial. "Pho has been looking forward to this."

Her stomach turned at the lie. Luis' sharp gaze fell on her as he stepped forward, taking her hand in his. He kissed it with exaggerated flourish, his dark eyes boring into hers.

"My sweet, it's a pleasure to see you again," he said softly.

Pho forced a stiff smile, barely suppressing a cringe. She hated being addressed as *my sweet* – the words dripped with possession.

"Luis," she said, her voice barely above a whisper. "How have you been?"

"Ah, she speaks at last!" he teased, his laughter too loud for her liking. "Come, let us walk."

Reluctantly, she matched his pace as he guided her through the bustling streets. They stopped at a narrow alley where a street vendor displayed a collection of garments.

"Five hundred baht for a coat!" the elderly vendor croaked, his bony hands gesturing to a fine leopard-fur coat. "A fine gentleman like you wouldn't let your lady go cold, would you?"

Luis chuckled, reaching into his pocket. "Of course not! But let's not be hasty. Will you accept four hundred?"

The vendor's eyes gleamed with amusement. "Four hundred and fifty, and it's yours."

"Done," Luis replied, and he handed over the money with practiced ease, taking the coat and draping it over Pho's shoulders. The fur was incredibly soft, its black spots striking against the vibrant orange.

"Let this coat symbolize our love," Luis declared, pressing another kiss to her hand.

Pho stiffened. While the coat's warmth was appreciated, the overt theatrics grated on her nerves.

As they continued down the alley, Luis' spending spree only intensified. Trinkets, baubles, and exotic foods passed from vendors to his hands, most of which he presented to Pho with an air of grandiosity. His carefree disregard for money was as ostentatious as his polished boots.

"Come, my sweet!" Luis called, holding up a wedge of brie. "Let us enjoy this at the seaside while we watch the waves."

Pho nodded reluctantly, her lips pressed into a thin line. His expression faltered as he studied her face.

"Are you well, my love?" he asked, his voice tinged with concern. "You seem… reserved."

"I'm fine," Pho replied curtly. "Let's go."

Her clipped response sailed past him unnoticed, as he eagerly took her hand again. Together, they began the trek down the main street of Phārā, the distant sound of the sea beckoning. Each step felt heavier to Pho, the weight of her own uncertainty pressing down harder than the fine coat on her shoulders.

The streets of the village were lively, filled with the chatter of merchants and the vibrant hum of a market day. The sharp tang of saltwater mingled with the scent of sizzling street food, but Pho barely noticed. Her thoughts churned, her focus drawn inward as Luis chatted on, oblivious to her discomfort.

When they finally reached the seaside, the view was breathtaking. Waves crashed against the shore, their foamy crests sparkling under the midday sun. The beach stretched wide and inviting, scattered with families, fishermen, and children chasing kites. Luis led her to a shaded spot beneath a canopy of palm trees, where a blanket had already been laid out, no doubt by one of his many attendants.

"Isn't it perfect?" Luis exclaimed, spreading his arms as if to claim the view as his own. "A setting worthy of our union."

Pho sat down stiffly, her hands gripping the edge of the blanket. The sea was beautiful, but it felt distant, as though she could not fully connect to its vast freedom while seated beside him.

Luis unpacked the items he had purchased, arranging them in a meticulous display. The wedge of brie sat in the center, accompanied by crackers, fresh fruits, and a small bottle of wine.

"Pho," Luis began, his tone suddenly serious. He moved closer, leaning in as though he were about to share a great secret. "I know this may feel overwhelming. The preparations, the expectations – but you'll see. Life with me will be everything you've ever dreamed of."

She hesitated, unsure of how to respond. The wind tugged at her hair, a fleeting reminder of the freedom she craved. "It's... a lot to take in," she admitted, keeping her voice even.

Luis reached out, brushing a strand of hair from her face. "You'll adapt," he said with a reassuring smile that felt more like a command. It made Pho feel numb. "In Belrance, you'll have every luxury. Servants to attend to your needs, a home fit for a queen – my queen." He paused. "Perhaps one day, if I am to be granted the title of Xudm by the King, we shall rule together. I am used to getting my way, you know."

Pho forced another smile but said nothing. His last few words felt like a threat. Her eyes drifted to the horizon, where the waves met the sky. She wondered how far she could sail if she just stepped into one of the fishing boats moored nearby. How far would she need to go to reclaim herself?

Luis poured two glasses of wine, handing one to her. "To us," he said, raising his glass.

Pho hesitated, then lifted hers. "To us," she said quietly.

She took a small sip, the taste of the wine rich and heavy. As Luis launched into another monologue about their future, her thoughts wandered. She imagined an escape route, some way out of her current situation.

A voice interrupted her daydream. "Miss?"

It was soft, almost hesitant. She turned to see a young boy standing a few feet away, holding a bundle of small purple flowers. His clothes were tattered, and he looked as though he had been running.

"These are for you," the boy said, his wide eyes darting nervously toward Luis.

Luis' smile froze. "Who sent you, boy?" he asked sharply.

"No one, sir," the boy stammered. "I found these flowers by the cliffs. I thought they'd be nice for the lady."

Pho reached for the flowers, her heart softening at the gesture. "Thank you," she said warmly.

Luis loomed over the boy. "Next time, you'll ask permission before disturbing us, understood?"

The boy nodded quickly and ran off, leaving Pho clutching the flowers. She looked up at Luis, her earlier warmth fading under his cold gaze.

"They're just flowers," she said quietly.

Luis sighed, sitting back down. "You'll learn soon enough. There's a proper order to things. Even small disruptions must be addressed."

Pho held the flowers tightly, her knuckles whitening. She stared at the petals, delicate and wild, and thought about how easily they could be crushed.

Chapter Three

The sun glinted off the golden gates of Boron Nigh as Drew returned to the capital – not as a cadet, but as a hero. A year ago, these streets had bled rebellion. Now, they gleamed with peace. In his stead was Josh and Geetie Gunnersbury, his two friends clearly enjoying the sunshine. A call of welcome sounded and Naz, Chief of the New Protectors of Harleland, came down to receive them. Drew put up his hand in welcome.

"It is good to see you again, my friends!" called Naz.

"We'd never miss a party like this!" Geetie grinned. "I even lugged my instruments all the way from the manor – my trusty Lyre included."

Naz laughed. "It wouldn't have been a proper party without you, Geetie. Now come! The King awaits!"

"Always has to steal the show," Josh whispered to Drew, a smirk on his face.

"Of course," Drew laughed, looking at his apprentice in amusement. "Your father isn't your father unless he's entertaining someone!"

Together, the four friends walked through the clean streets of Boron Nigh. It was almost like the great rebellion of a year ago had never occurred. Save for some cracks here and there, all evidence of the battle between the Uprising movement and the group of rebel Protectors that Naz had led had all been swept away.

They passed the East Bay Protector Unit, the largest unit of Protectors in Harleland, which was next to the eastern gate of the city. Drew's heart fluttered as he stared through those gates and out toward Lekt Valley. Somewhere in that valley lay his home village of Dempair. Soon, they arrived at the great staircase that led to Palace Rock, the top part of the city of Boron Nigh where the Royal Family lived.

As they ascended the stairs, suits of living armour seemed to stare directly into Drew's soul. He had been terrified of them the first time he had come to Palace Rock, over a year and a half ago. But now he felt welcomed by them. Soon, the four friends made it to the top of the stairs and stepped out into the main square of Palace Rock.

"Hail, Saran!" called a voice. It was a voice that belonged to King Lekt the Second, ruler of Harleland. He approached the newcomers, a glass of sparkling prosecco in his left hand.

"My Lord," said Naz in welcome as he bowed.

As Drew went to bow, Lekt stopped him. "My friend," he began. "You bow to no one! You are the saviour of Harleland." He chortled. "I should be the one bowing to you!"

"Well Josh!" began Geetie. "Bow to King Drew!"

Josh rolled his eyes.

Drew laughed. "I appreciate the kindness, my Lord," he said. "And a big congratulations on your first anniversary as King!"

Lekt shook his head. "My anniversary is not what we are celebrating, my friend." He turned back towards the party and loudly exclaimed: "Today we celebrate one year since the end of the war with the Crownlands, and the defeat of the Uprising movement!"

A loud chorus of cheers went up amongst all present.

Lekt turned back to Drew, Josh and Geetie, as Naz departed to mingle with some of the Protectors on the other side of the square.

Geetie looked around. "There's two of us missing!" he declared. "Where are Octavia and Tenebrae?"

Lekt suddenly looked sullen.

"As much as this is a party atmosphere," said the King, his tone turning serious. "There is one vital piece of information I must share with you all."

Drew stared at him, confused. Was it something to do with the Crownlands? He exchanged a look with Geetie and Josh, who also seemed concerned.

Lekt shepherded the trio into a quiet corner. He looked at them with concern.

"Octavia is gravely ill," he announced.

"Oh," replied Josh. "Like… how ill?"

Lekt looked down at the ground. "The physicians say that nothing they have done seems to be working. They believe he has contracted pneumonia, perhaps as a result of his shoulder injury he suffered when he fought Renault."

"But I used the runes to cure his shoulder," replied Drew in confusion.

Lekt shook his head. "Apparently some sort of injury persisted," he explained. "How it has got this bad, the physicians cannot say."

"How long has it been since he became ill?" asked Geetie.

"Octavia's wife, Summer, took him to the hospital around a month ago," explained Lekt. "He was coughing up blood and complained that his shoulder ache had worsened."

"Can we see him?" asked Drew.

Lekt shrugged. "You can, but he won't be very talkative. He hasn't spoken a word in over a week." His voice changed to a whisper. "You may need to be prepared to say goodbye."

Drew's eyes widened. A tear began to form in his right eye. No. This could not be right. Octavia was old, yes, but he still had many years left to enjoy his retirement, surely.

"I want to see him now," said Drew, his mind feeling distant.

Lekt sighed. "Of course," he agreed. "Follow me."

***

Drew felt sick. The jolly mood he and the others shared earlier had all but vanished, and now a feeling of worry seemed to hang over their heads. King Lekt led Drew, Geetie and Josh to the hospital, a grand old building that stood not far from the entrance to the staircase at the base of Palace Rock. The hospital had, thankfully, been spared any major damage during the Revolt of Boron Nigh the previous year despite its close proximity to the upper half of the city. The group entered and were greeted by a nurse.

"My Lord," she said, staring in awe at King Lekt as she bowed.

"We are here to see Octavia," said the King.

"Of course," replied the nurse. "He has two visitors with him already though, so do not be long. I don't want to overwhelm him."

"Of course," agreed the King. He looked at Drew, Geetie and Josh. "Come," he said, waving them forward. "This way."

They followed the nurse, who led them up to the top level of the hospital. There in a grand room overlooking the city was Octavia, laying asleep in a large bed. Beside him was his wife Summer, and to Drew's surprise, Tenebrae sat beside the old Protector on his other side. Joy appeared on her face when she saw Drew and the others.

"Tenebrae!" called Geetie and Josh together, as Drew went over to meet her.

"It's good to see you again!" said Drew.

"Same here," replied Tenebrae. She looked at Octavia in concern. "He's dying, Drew," she whispered. "I went to visit

Octavia at his new home in Cernsland, but he wasn't there. I travelled here after some of his friends told me what had happened."

Drew felt sullen. He could not let this happen. Not when he had the runes. Approaching the ill man, Drew withdrew one of the green Life Runes. Placing his hand on Octavia's shoulder, he muttered:

Devine.

The air in the room shifted. The light dimmed, as though a cloud had passed overhead. Drew felt the rune vibrate against his palm. Suddenly, Octavia opened his eyes. But they seemed… cold. Empty. Different. Slowly, his head turned toward Drew, his eyes opened wide, unblinking. Drew shuddered. Something was giving him the creeps. He barely noticed the others all moving closer to witness what was unfolding.

"Beyond the sea," began Octavia. "There is a jewel. A jewel that must be obtained lest evil gets its way."

Drew stared at Octavia wide eyed. He looked at the others. Summer leant down and tried to comfort her ill husband.

"Please, my love. Just rest," she whispered.

But Octavia ignored her and continued speaking to Drew.

"Only the Ocean Sapphire can cure me now," he announced. "You must find it, Saran. Before…" he began to trail off. "…he does."

Octavia closed his eyes and his head rolled back. The old Protector was fast asleep again.

"What did you do to him!" cried Summer, staring at Drew accusingly.

"I…" muttered Drew, but he could not get the words out.

"I think," began Tenebrae. "That we should leave Octavia and Summer alone."

"I agree," replied Geetie. "Let's go."

They left the hospital, King Lekt casting glances towards Drew, clearly with a million things to say. Drew sighed. He supposed he should get the conversation over and done with, although he wanted to talk with Geetie, Josh and Tenebrae about this in private. Without King Lekt butting in.

"What do you know about the Ocean Sapphire, Drew?" asked Lekt.

Drew shrugged. "I've heard of it. They told us about it when I was young back in the orphanage. Apparently, the ancient Kings of Nearth kept it as a symbol of their power."

Lekt nodded. "The Ocean Sapphire is said to be formed of the Weather Runes," he explained.

Drew stopped in his tracks. "The Weather Runes?" he echoed.

"Yes," answered Lekt matter-of-factly. "I mean… you already have the Shadow Runes from my father, the Life Runes from Wilder Forest… I assume you would have started looking for the Weather Runes anyway, at some point."

Drew nodded. "Duchess Wilder told me it was my destiny to find and master all of the runes," he explained.

"Then if you do set out to find the Ocean Sapphire, you go with my blessing," said Lekt. He smiled. "Like you wouldn't have gone anyway even if I didn't give you my blessing!"

Drew laughed. "I'd already be on my way!" he said. "But I must speak to my friends now. We need to decide what to do."

Lekt nodded. "Of course," he said. Then he stopped, as if pondering something. "Who do you think Octavia meant by *he*? Find the Ocean Sapphire before *he* does…"

Drew felt a wave of fear flicker through him. Perhaps there was another out there looking for the runes?

He turned from the King, his mind racing. If someone else was hunting the Ocean Sapphire… the race had already begun. He went to join his friends. There was much to discuss.

Chapter Four

"I don't think you understand what's at stake here, Pho," Chip snapped, his voice rising with desperation.

Her father was giving her a lecture about how good it would be for their family if she agreed to marry Luis. She stared at the ground, her anger slowly rising.

"Finally we will have status! We can live in luxury! And at the moment you're being selfish!" he cried.

Pho looked up and found her courage. "Selfish?" she yelled. "The way I see it, *you* are the only one of us three who wants this so-called 'luxury' and 'status.'" She paused. Chip looked shocked at her outburst. "You know what? I don't think you've *ever* considered my opinion!" she continued.

"Well–" stammered Chip. "I-I… I have before!" He rolled his eyes up as if thinking. "I let you decorate the kitchen!"

Pho stared back flabbergasted. "I got to do some interior design?" she screeched. "That's the best you can come up with?"

Then Chip's eyes narrowed. "I let you scatter the last of your grandmother's – my mother's – ashes after she passed last year," he said quietly. "That is the greatest honour a father can give to his children."

Pho took a step back. She looked around a bit, unsure of what to do. And then she ran. She ran out of the house, ignoring her father's cries, and made her way swiftly through

the village toward the seaside. Her mind raced. Perhaps her
father was right. Perhaps she was being selfish.

After a few minutes, she arrived at the beach. The waves
crashed against the shore, and the smell of sea spray hit her
nose. Sullen, Pho walked up the beach unsure of what to do
next. Go back? What would going back achieve? Her
mother, although sympathetic, was often supportive of her
father. She realised with a jolt that she had no one. No
friends to speak of, and her family wanted only what was in
their interests for her. Pho was truly alone.

"Excuse me, miss!" called a familiar voice.

Pho turned and recognised the boy from the day before. She
smiled at him. "Thanks for those flowers yesterday!" she
called, as he approached.

"Are you okay?" he asked. "I saw you run down from the
village. I'm called Hax."

Hax held out his hand and Pho took it. "I'm Pho!" she
replied.

The boy looked no older than ten, and Pho was unsure why
he was down on the beach by himself.

"Where are your parents?" she asked.

Hax shrugged. "My father died when I was young," he
admitted. "My mother and I moved here to Phārā just the
other week." He paused. "I'm just looking for new friends."

Pho smiled. "I'll be your friend!" she announced.

"I'd like that," he replied. "Oh, but… I hope your husband doesn't mind. He didn't seem to like me very much."

"Oh, he's not my husband!" laughed Pho. Then she stopped, and a look of sadness came over her face. "At least not yet."

"You don't seem to like him very much," said Hax. "My mother always says – surround yourself with people you love!"

"I wish it were that easy," she replied.

"Come over here!" Hax called. "I found something cool in one of the caves!"

Pho hesitated, then nodded. A beach adventure might clear her head. She followed the boy to the entrance to a small cave in the side of the seacliff that towered over the beach.

"Follow, follow!" he called excitedly.

Pho followed, but she began to grow concerned by the fact that the walls of the cave seemed to press closer together the deeper they went.

"Be careful, Hax," she called. "We don't want to get stuck in here."

"It's fine!" called Hax. "I explored here yesterday!"

Although concerned for the child's wellbeing, she agreed to continue walking deeper. Suddenly, the passage ended and the duo emerged into a small cavern. Sunlight filtered down through shafts in the roof and reflected off the light sandstone walls. Then she noticed it. Sticking halfway out of the sand was a blue, glowing jewel. Hax went over to it and picked the jewel up.

"Isn't this cool?" he exclaimed. "It's the most beautiful thing I've ever seen! I couldn't believe it when I found it yesterday."

Pho stared at it in wonder. Hax was right, this glowing gemstone was incredible. Light danced off the surface of the stone, and when held in the light of the shaft, it seemed to make the entire cavern glow blue. Hax handed her the jewel, and she studied it.

"It looks like sapphire," she murmured, turning it in her hand. "But… not like any I've seen before."

She went to hand it back to Hax, but he shook his head. "I want you to have it!" he declared. "It's my gift to you."

"Oh, Hax," she said. "That is very sweet of you, but you gave me those flowers yesterday! I couldn't possibly ask for anything else."

"Maybe this will help cheer you up!" Hax replied.

Pho went to reply, but suddenly she noticed the light from the shaft was fading and it began to feel cold.

"I think a storm might be brewing," she said. "We should go."

Hax nodded. "I agree," he said. "Race you to the village!"

Pho laughed. "You're on!" she declared.

Together, the two friends walked back down the tunnel and back onto the beach. Pho was taken aback at just how dark the sky had gotten. Black storm clouds brewed on the horizon, making the ocean below churn.

"We'd better hurry!" she called above the rising winds. She checked she had the blue jewel tucked safely in her robes, and then began to run, Hax beside her as the rain began to pour down. A flash of lightning split the sky – then came the loudest thunderclap Pho had ever heard. She screwed her eyes shut, and when she opened them, she was shocked to see a ditch had been formed in the sand beside her. Hax pulled her arm.

"Faster!" he cried over the storm. "That lightning bolt nearly struck you!"

Fear began rising in Pho. Suddenly, another bolt of lightning seemed to strike just meters away, accompanied by a deafening BOOM! She and Hax began to run, making for the village as the storm raged around them. Lightning struck around them as the two friends ran on. Finally, the village was before them.

"Look, Chip!" called a voice. "There she is!"

"Pho!" screamed Chip, as he stood beside a fellow villager watching her and Hax sprint for the safety of the village.

All of a sudden, another BOOM and flash of light, and the next thing Pho knew, she was hurtling through the air and then saw and felt no more.

***

"Darling, are you okay?" the soft, soothing voice of Pho's mother, Thu, reached her ears. She tried to open her eyes, finally forcing her eyelids open and looking around. She was in a bed in the medicine hut, the village physician standing over her, while her parents stood together on the other side of the bed.

"Mother!" Pho cried. Thu smiled at her daughter. Pho looked over at her father.

"I'm glad you're okay," he said. "You should not have run off like that! We searched and searched and–"

"Save it for later, Chip," warned Thu. "Let her rest."

Chip sighed. "Of course."

"You're very lucky you didn't break your neck," explained the physician. "That lightning bolt struck just behind you, and the force lifted you up and threw you a good five meters."

Pho's heart caught in her throat. She could have been crippled. Then another thought came into her mind. Hax!

"Is the boy I was with, Hax, okay?" she asked.

"Oh, him?" replied Chip. "We sent him away to his mother so he would stop bothering us."

Pho's resentment toward her father returned. "He would have only been trying to help!" she replied.

"Who is he anyway?" her father asked. "I've seen him around the last week or so, perhaps he's new. Apparently he keeps getting in everyone's way."

"He's just trying to make friends," explained Pho.

"Well, you're soon to be a married woman," Chip explained. "You don't have time to be making friends with children. Speaking of married. Luis will come to see you this afternoon! He was worried sick when we informed him of what had happened."

Oh, great, thought Pho. Just what she wanted. Luis.

"Ohh, I'm not feeling good," Pho lied. "I wouldn't want Luis to see me like this."

"A man must be there for his woman in sickness and in health," explained Chip. "Luis is no exception!"

"I think she just wants to be left alone for a while," said Thu.

Chip sighed. "So be it. We'll give you some space before Luis arrives later on."

With that, her parents departed. Pho grabbed her pillow, put it on her face and screamed into it. The physician stared at her.

"Um… everything okay, miss?" he asked.

Pho looked at him. "Please don't admit Luis to see me," she begged. "He's the last person I want to see."

The physician looked at her warmly. "I will see what I can do," he said. "But sometimes it is unwise to stand in front of what a Belrench Commander wants."

And there it is again, she thought. *Belrench will over everything else.*

Pho sighed. She was doomed to be trapped in here with Luis this afternoon, she could feel it.

Suddenly, a memory came back to her. She felt in her robe, and sure enough, her hand collided with the smooth surface of the glowing blue jewel that she and Hax had found earlier. Waiting for the physician to go, Pho pulled the gemstone out. The sapphire dripped with power. She suppressed a gasp. Did this thing attract the lightning bolts? Had this strange jewel saved her… or tried to kill her?

Chapter Five

Tenebrae sat in a leather chair by the fireplace as Drew listened to her tale, and Geetie and Josh sat together in their own chairs a little way off.

"I've struggled to fit in around Boron Nigh," she admitted. "I left and travelled to Cernsland, to discover myself."

Drew nodded, understanding all too well. He and Tenebrae had once shared something deeper – though now, their paths seemed oceans apart. He thought back to their discussion, a year ago, as they walked back to Wilder Forest from the border with the Crownlands. They had agreed to be just friends, however Drew barely felt like he knew her anymore. She was always travelling, sometimes going months without returning to Boron Nigh. It felt good to see her again, and Drew allowed himself to enjoy the warmth of the fireplace as they sat in the orphanage back in Dempair.

He awkwardly tilted his head, weighing up his next words. "I'm glad we could still be together, as friends," he said finally, lowering his voice. "I mean, we promised each other in the Great Tower."

Tenebrae nodded. She smiled. "So am I," she said.

Geetie, the orphanage master, sat in silence as he too listened to Tenebrae. For the past fourteen months, he had been in charge of the orphanage after taking over from Phil and Julia Fisher. Drew sometimes wondered what had happened to them. Julia was always an unpleasant old witch, but Phil was at least somewhat tolerable, even if a little gruff sometimes.

"I've missed you all," continued Tenebrae. "But it seems like I'm back in time to help figure out what this Ocean Sapphire business is all about."

Drew nodded. It was time to get down to business.

"King Lekt said the Ocean Sapphire is known to him and the Kingdom's wisemen," he explained. "But nobody knows anything about it other than the fact that it is made up of the five Weather Runes."

"If it was once the symbol of the ancient Kings of Nearth," added Geetie. "Then I imagine it would be nigh on impossible to locate."

"I agree," said Tenebrae. "No one knows where the ancient Kings even lived. If we knew that, perhaps we would know where to start."

"The fact it's called the Ocean Sapphire tells me the ocean is a good place to start," suggested Josh.

"There's a lot of seas around Harleland," replied Drew. "We'd be searching for a long time."

"Why don't we ask Kora?" suggested Tenebrae.

Drew nodded. He had thought about the Dragon of Hoonth, living in her cave within the Dirtgula Mountains. He knew that Naz had visited her alongside the Witch of Cold Valley during his exile.

"I think it's a good start," he agreed.

"When should we set off?" asked Josh.

"As soon as possible I should think," suggested Geetie. "The sooner we can find this jewel and save Octavia, the better."

"Just as long as we don't run into whoever *he* is, that Octavia warned us about," said Josh. "Any clues as to who that might be?"

"Shârvous?" pondered Tenebrae. "I mean, he still refuses to give back control of Canterbury, who's to say he's not still making other schemes behind the scenes?"

"Perhaps," answered Drew. "His right-hand man, my uncle, Count Michael, knows I can wield runes."

"There must surely be many other bad actors in this world other than Shârvous," Geetie pointed out. "We should keep an open mind."

"Then it's settled," said Drew. "We'll go see Kora." He looked at his friends. "Who's coming?"

"I think we all are," said Tenebrae.

"Agreed," added Geetie. "I wouldn't miss this for the world!"

"Our friend is dying," said Josh. "This quest belongs to all of us."

Warmth flooded through Drew. Geetie, Josh and Tenebrae would all accompany him to the Dirtgula Mountains. And perhaps even beyond to find the Ocean Sapphire.

***

The four companions set out early the next morning from
Dempair.

As they said their goodbyes, Geetie had made one of Drew's
childhood friends, Hermit, the acting orphanage master in his
stead.

"You can count on me, as always," Hermit had said.

"I should hope so," answered Drew with a smirk.

Hermit laughed. "It will be a big workload to be fair," he
admitted. "Now that I'm the new bull herder and all."

"Not exactly new anymore," replied Drew. "You've been
Hermit the Bull Herder for the past three months!"

"Being the new guy comes with its perks," answered Hermit.

"When it suits you," said Drew. "You were boasting to me
after just a month in the job that you were the best bull
herder Dempair had ever seen!"

"What does a bull herder even do?" asked Josh.

"We herd bulls," replied Hermit. "It's in the name! They're
important to Dempair's micro-economy."

"But why bulls?" replied Josh. "Cows? Sheep? That'd make
more sense, surely."

"Beef from bulls is very protein-rich," replied Geetie, as he
packed the very meat in his bag.

All present chortled at Josh and Hermit's discussion.

They said their goodbyes to Hermit and set off, climbing out of Lekt Valley via the eastern road toward Dirtgula. This was a much less travelled road due to the lack of trade between Lekt Valley and Dirtgula. The road was rocky and steep, and Geetie managed to hurt his ankle at some point.

"Blast this road," Geetie declared, irritated. "That useless oaf Duke Barnshire really ought to fix his roads."

"I don't think Barnshire really cares about anyone but himself," answered Drew, remembering back to the first time he had met his Dutchy's Lord. The way Barnshire had spoken to King Lakton when he first met Drew in the orphanage fourteen months prior showed his lack of respect and selfish character.

"The slimy little runt certainly knew how to lay low during the Uprising movement business," said Tenebrae.

"He's a political opportunist, just like Count Balnather was," answered Geetie. "My business dealings with Duke Barnshire have been nothing short of unpleasant."

The company walked on in silence. It was midday when Drew halted the company and declared they should rest for lunch.

"Anyone for sausages?" asked Geetie, already pulling out his camp stove and a rope of fresh sausages.

"Mmm, yes please!" answered Josh.

"We have four pork and four beef," explained Geetie. "One flavour each!"

The food merchant set up his stove and began cooking lunch.
Tenebrae sat down next to Drew, while Josh hungrily looked
at the sizzling meats on the saucepan.

"Do you know exactly where in the mountains Kora lives?"
Tenebrae asked.

Drew shrugged. "According to Naz, it was a cave filled with
glow worms that overlooked Cold Valley."

"We could always see the Witch?" she suggested. "She
could lead us to Kora."

"The Witch probably won't want to be disturbed," answered
Drew. "And besides, we would have to climb down the
mountains and then into the valley, just to climb all the way
back up again."

"I agree," added Josh, joining Drew and Tenebrae. "It will
be quicker to find her on our own."

Geetie finished cooking their sausages and the four
companions ate together merrily, chatting about this and that.
After they finished, Drew and Josh found a nearby stream to
wash up the plates before the company got ready to depart.

As they washed the plates, Drew could not help noticing the
beauty of the mountains surrounding them. The range
seemed to get taller and taller as they went on, with the
majority of the Dirtgula Mountains forming the Dutchy
border between Dirtgula and Lekt Valley in the south, the
Greenarch Plain in the middle and the Crownlands in the
north. The peaks above Cold Valley were snow-capped,
towering like ancient sentinels. Every now and again, a hawk

or falcon would fly lazily high above them, searching for small rodents that lived in the grassy tufts that were scattered all over the mountains. And the view! The view from where Drew and the company stood was breathtaking. They could see the entire Greenarch Plain stretching northward, with a faint glimpse of the River Harl on the horizon which marked the border with the Crownlands.

"I think we've rested for long enough," Josh declared.

Drew nodded in agreement. "The quicker we can find Kora, the quicker we can save Octavia."

"How much time do you think he has?" asked Tenebrae. "What if we're too late?"

Geetie's usually jolly face turned into a look of fear and sadness, and he stared at the ground.

"Weeks, maybe," whispered Drew. "I feel as though he will hold on for as long as possible, but…" He trailed off.

"Let's go then!" declared Josh. "By nightfall we should be halfway there!"

Tenebrae gave him a supportive smile. She was clearly buoyed by his enthusiasm. Drew was impressed by his leadership.

"Okay," he decided. "Let's move on."

Chapter Six

"Make way!" called the voice of Commander Luis. "Do not stand between my lady and I!"

The physician cast a sorry glance towards Pho as Luis came barging into the room. He stared at her longingly.

"My love!" he said with concern, rushing to her side. "How are you feeling? I'm sorry I'm late, I came as soon as I heard the news. Alas, for I was hunting in the meadows about an hour's ride away."

"Oh, that's fine," answered Pho nonchalantly.

Luis took her hand and kissed it. Pho cringed. To her relief, the physician stood just a few meters away.

"I am glad you're okay," said Luis. "If something worse were to happen to you, I don't think I could have forgiven myself for not being there to protect you." Then, a look of anger came over his face. "I heard something about that boy actually," he continued. "Apparently he was leading you off down the beach! I shall have a good word to him and his parents – stay away from my Pho!"

"He's a nice, sweet boy!" Pho argued. "He's new to town and just wants friends."

"Well he can find someone from his class to be friends with," answered Luis. "People like us shall associate themselves with fellow high-class individuals."

Luis' words made Pho sick.

"Your so-called 'classes' are elitist and horrible," she declared. "Hax is a human just like me and you."

"My love, you need to accept my judgments and my decisions," Luis declared. "From this day on I forbid you to hang around with Hax. If I see you two together, I shall arrange for him and his family to be moved to another village."

Pho stared at Luis in cold dislike. The Commander seemed to take no heed of her body language and instead stood, said goodbye, and departed. She looked desperately at the physician.

"Help me," she begged.

The physician looked at her in sympathy. "Commander Luis usually gets what he wants," he said. "I have seen many people in Phārā try to stand up to him. Each time, he manages to find ways to ruin their reputation and they have no choice but to leave for another village."

"I just wish I could have my parents on my side," Pho admitted. "My father doesn't seem to care about anyone but himself, and my mother seems unwilling to stand up to him."

The physician sighed. "I wish I could do more to help," he said.

Pho sighed. She rolled onto her side and tried to rest.

***

"Pssst!"

Pho stared across the dark hospital room in the direction of the noise. There was someone hiding under the bench by the far wall!

"Hello?" she whispered.

Out from under the bench came the familiar figure of Hax. What was he doing here, and at this time of night?

"Hax?" asked Pho. "You shouldn't be here! If Commander Luis sees you…"

"It's okay!" said Hax. "I'm not scared of that big oaf!"

Pho smiled at the boy's bravery.

"I'm here to make sure you're okay!" he said. "They wouldn't let me in this afternoon, and I got told off by that big oaf as he walked in."

Pho remembered Luis' warning earlier that day, to move Hax and his family to another village if the boy was seen interacting with Pho again.

"Hax, you could get yourself in a lot of trouble," Pho explained. "Even your family could be affected."

"Why are you even with him?" asked Hax. "I heard you're marrying him."

Pho sighed. "I am expected to marry a man of high-class," she explained. "My father arranged it. It will give my family standing."

"But he's not a very nice man," said Hax matter-of-factly.

Pho almost laughed. "No, he's not," she said. "But I have no choice."

"We all have a choice," said Hax. "Well, that's what my mother says anyway."

"Your mother says a lot of things," said Pho.

"Well, yeah, I guess," replied Hax. "She was the wise woman in our old village, before we got kicked out by the Belrench Commander in charge." A look of sadness came over his face. "My mother gave him a prophecy he didn't like, and he punished us by exiling us. So we moved here."

"Your mother gives prophecies?" asked Pho.

"Well, yes," answered Hax. "For a fee, of course." He looked at her guiltily. "We have to make money somehow."

Pho laughed. "And how much would it cost for a psychic reading from her?"

"Hmm," answered Hax. "I'm sure when she finds out that we're friends she'll give you a discount!"

Pho's interest was piqued. "Maybe she can tell me about this jewel here," she wondered, pulling out the glowing blue gemstone. "I wonder if this truly did cause the lightning to try and strike me."

"It looked like the storm was chasing you," said Hax. He paused. "When are you coming out of here?"

"Tomorrow, ideally," answered Pho.

"Cool!" said Hax. "I'll arrange a session for you tomorrow afternoon!"

"But Hax," said Pho. "Remember what Luis said... if he sees you around me again, you and your mother will be in deep trouble."

She did not want to tell him that he would likely be moved once more to another village. He was just a boy, and she did not want to frighten him.

"It's okay!" said Hax. "Meet me in the dunes behind the beach, mid-afternoon tomorrow! We'll be out of sight of anyone in the village or on the beach. Then I'll lead you to our abode!"

Pho thought for a moment. "Okay," she said. "Let's do it."

Excitement came over Hax's face. "Okay!" he said. "Good luck tomorrow morning! And I'll be seeing you."

With that, Hax snuck over to the window and slipped out. Pho smiled. She had made a friend. She finally had someone who agreed that Luis was a bad influence in her life. She felt happiness well up inside her. And excitement. What secrets would Hax's mother reveal tomorrow afternoon?

Chapter Seven

"I never thought I'd be back at this place."

Geetie looked down into the misty vale of Cold Valley as Drew, Tenebrae and Josh stood on a precipice. Drew knew that somewhere down there, far under the misty veil, lived Horath, the Witch of Cold Valley. He looked up. He also knew that, far above them in a cave within the mountains, lived Kora the Dragon.

The four companions stood on an outcrop overlooking the valley. Memories of the journey through the vale flooded back to Drew, the cold, muddy path and the impenetrable mist. He and the others, as well as Octavia, had braved Cold Valley on the quest to the Great Tower of Hoonth. He remembered with a shudder being led astray thanks to the Witch's visions, which included seeing a vision of his mother, San, causing him to wade out into the bottomless pit of mud. He sighed as he remembered his mother. He had eventually met her for real not long after, in the frosty land of Wiln, far over the sea. She had been the leader of a tribe of Vikings who lived in Wiln, however after her death in the Great Tower, leadership of the tribe had fallen to Drew. He still meant to go back there one day, but he knew the tribe was in the safe hands of his chosen acting leader, Rørth.

"Do you think Kora's cave will be around here somewhere?" asked Josh, coming up beside Drew.

"Naz said it overlooked Cold Valley," explained Drew. "It must be one of the caves nearby."

"I see no entrances anywhere," said Tenebrae, scanning the grey boulders behind them.

"Well, a magic dragon probably lives in a magic cave," said Geetie. "Perhaps the entrance will reveal itself to us."

Drew suddenly had an idea. He took out his rune bag and rummaged around for the right one. Five dark, stone runes of shadow and five green, leaf runes of life; but would one of these runes reveal the location of Kora's cave?

Drew held one of the Life Runes in his hand and spoke.

See.

Suddenly, he was swept off his feet and he seemed to be gazing down upon the Dirtgula Mountains from above. He seemed to be able to see right through them! Wait. There! He could see a small cavern deep within the mountain his friends now stood upon. Two purple eyes seemed to appear in the cavern and stared straight up at him. He knew they could see him, and then came the voice.

At sunset, my runes will reveal the entrance, it said.

Drew was then thrown back to the ground and he stood before Geetie, Josh and Tenebrae like nothing had ever happened.

"Are you okay Drew?" asked Tenebrae. "You seemed to be in a trance for a bit there."

"Oh, uh," stuttered Drew. "I'm okay. I think I know how to get into the cave now, though!"

They set up a small camp in the shadow of the great grey boulders. Josh had decided to climb to the top of the boulders to get a better view of the world below them. He had come back with a smile on his face, declaring happily that he had walked up further to the snow.

"Still young at heart," said Geetie with relief. "I don't want my boy to grow up too fast."

Drew looked at the food merchant in sadness. "I guess we've all had to grow up faster than we wanted to," he said.

"I was lucky," explained Geetie. "My childhood back in the isles of the Outer Dirtgulas was more than any child could ask for."

They spent the rest of the afternoon sitting around their small camp, eating a light afternoon tea prepared by Geetie. Tenebrae had helped too, causing Geetie to declare her as his sous chef.

"When all this is over, Tenebrae and I will go into business together!" declared Geetie with glee. "G&T's Pub! Together we can create some of the most *marvelous* meals!"

Drew and Josh laughed together as they thought of Geetie and Tenebrae working in a kitchen together.

"I may need a few more cooking lessons to be fair," admitted Tenebrae with a smile.

They ate and laughed until the sun began to set. Drew almost choked on his lamb chop as he realised time was running out to locate Kora's cave. He quickly reached into his rune bag and took out the five Shadow Runes. He remembered what the dragon had said – her runes would reveal the entrance. He decided that she must have meant the Shadow Runes, which like her, were from Hoonth.

"Do you think it will work?" asked Tenebrae with worry.

"Of course it will work," said Josh. "It's got too."

Drew held the five dark rune stones out in front of him. Nothing happened.

"Come on!" pleaded Drew. Thinking desperately, he decided to use each rune.

Shade.

A shadow passed over them all, but just as quickly, it vanished. Still nothing.

"Damn!" cursed Drew. He looked at another rune.

"Stand back," he warned, as his three friends all took steps away.

Kinetic.

A wave of kinetic energy pulsed from Drew, however, like with the *Shade* rune, nothing proceeded to happen. Drew shook his head in confusion.

"I just don't get it," he said. "Kora told me to use her runes at sunset!"

Just as he was about to give up, he noticed the Shadow
Runes had begun to glow a dim and faint purple. They
started to glow brighter, until they illuminated the entire
camp in a brilliant purple light. The four companions stared
at them in amazement.

"I didn't know the runes could do that," whispered Josh.

"Incredible," commented Geetie.

"Look!" called Tenebrae. "There's an opening in the
boulder!"

Sure enough, the light of the runes had revealed a cave
entrance in the side of the cliff face that they camped under.
When Drew moved the light away, the cave vanished.

"Only the light of the Shadow Runes can reveal the
entrance," said Josh in amazement.

"How whimsical!" said Geetie in excitement. "Drew, your
runes are full of surprises, that's for sure."

Drew began walking toward the entrance, Geetie, Josh and
Tenebrae in his stead. Together, the four companions entered
the secret cave.

***

Naz was absolutely correct about the glow worms. Drew
drew breath in amazement as he looked around at the
thousands of small blue lights that illuminated the cave.
Beside him, Geetie seemed to be turning in every direction
soaking in the magical atmosphere.

"In all my years…" he breathed. "When we return home, I shall dedicate all of my spare time to writing songs of the glow worms of Kora's cave!" He sighed. "If only I had arrived at Cold Valley earlier. I could have joined Naz and the others when they came here."

Drew recalled how Geetie had travelled to Cold Valley the year before, after Octavia warned him that Naz had been exiled from Boron Nigh by the Uprising movement. During his exile, Naz had visited Kora – in this very cave – alongside the Witch of Cold Valley, seeking guidance on how to defeat the movement. Geetie had arrived just after Naz returned, and together they had formed a plan to overthrow Count Balnather and reclaim Boron Nigh – a plan that, in the end, had succeeded.

Just then, a noise broke Drew from his thoughts. Two purple eyes appeared in the darkness before them, causing Josh to gasp and Tenebrae to take a step back. Not Drew though. He took a step forward, curiosity getting the better of his fear.

"Kora…" he breathed.

"We meet again Andrew Saran," replied a voice. The eyes started moving closer, and the glow worms illuminated the body of a great dragon, its black scales reflecting the dim light.

"We didn't mean to scare you off that day in Boron Nigh," said Drew, in awe of the beast before him. "I'm sorry."

Kora shook her head. "It was meant to be. Ker Gorûn decreed that the best gift he could impart upon Harleland was the gift of knowledge."

"So…" breathed Josh, coming in beside Drew. "You can talk?"

"I can do many things, Josh Gunnersbury," replied Kora. "But I sense the reason you have come here is not about my ability to talk."

Josh shrugged. "I suppose not," he said.

"Octavia…" started Drew.

"His illness is not caused by any natural circumstances," said Kora. "There is a reason he channeled the runes when you tried to heal him with them."

Drew gasped. "That's how he started talking about the Ocean Sapphire!"

Kora nodded her great head. "The runes are calling to each other," she explained. "The powers that be in the world have come to the realisation that only with all twenty runes assembled can the forces of evil be repelled."

"Evil?" asked Geetie. "But there's peace in Harleland now!"

"For now," warned Kora.

"Is this force of evil the same person looking for the runes that Octavia warned us about?" asked Drew. "And is it Shârvous?"

"These are irrelevant questions for the current situation," explained Kora. "You came here for guidance on where to find the Ocean Sapphire. For that, the Demi-gods have given me a prophecy." She paused.

Across a blue ocean, with many flows,

To Xudm's lands, an evil grows,

A child keeps the Ocean Sapphire,

But to end the dark, one must know,

Defeat the evil, and another will grow.

Tenebrae looked at Drew in annoyance. "They don't like giving clear instructions, do they?" she said.

Kora laughed. "I am but a messenger," she announced. "For this is how the Demi-gods speak. If I could give you the information in more concise terms I would." She sighed. "And now you must return to Boron Nigh and prepare for your quest!"

Drew nodded. "Thank you, Kora," he said. He turned to his friends. "I'm not sure I like the last part. About another evil growing."

"Until our next meeting, Andrew Saran," said the dragon.

With that, she withdrew into the darkness and closed her eyes, leaving the company alone with only the glow worms for company.

Chapter Eight

The breeze blew through Pho's long, dark hair as she walked
along the beach. Her father had been hard to convince to let
her go, however her mother had finally convinced him. To
them, Pho was having a nice little solo walk by the shore, a
way to forget the past day she had spent in the hospital after
the impact of the nearby lightning strike had flung her
through the air. She was still sore, but she was more excited
than anything – today she would get a psychic reading from
Hax's mother!

Once Pho was confident she was out of sight of the village,
she quickly turned and began to climb the sand dune beside
her, ready to see if Hax was indeed waiting on the other side
as they had agreed. As she reached the summit, she
happened to look down the beach. To her horror, none other
than Commander Luis could be seen some way off back
toward the village. She quickly dropped to the floor, not
caring about the mixture of sand and sharp thorns of the
dune plants. He was alone, it appeared, and that made Pho
even more alarmed. Had he seen her and followed her?
Usually he would be patrolling with fellow Belrench military
personnel. Quickly, she slid herself belly-first down the other
side of the dune. She nearly had a heart attack when she
heard someone speak up.

"Pho!" it said excitedly. "You're here!"

Pho looked up in fear, but fear was quickly replaced with
relief when she noticed Hax standing before her.

"Quickly, Hax," said Pho. "I saw Commander Luis back up the beach. We should move on from here, in case he's looking for me."

Hax nodded. "Okay," he agreed. "Follow me, I'll take you to my mother and I's house."

Pho followed Hax through the trees. The area behind the dunes was thick with them, making this the perfect spot to go to avoid being spotted by people like Luis. After a few minutes, Hax began to lead Pho back toward the village. Hax and his mother lived on the edge of town, which would mean getting inside would be easier for Pho then if they lived in the middle of the village. Soon, the trees began to thin out and Pho could see the village of Phārā. Built on the very edge of the treeline, an old run down shack could be seen, and Hax began to make a beeline straight for it.

"Here it is!" he declared proudly. "Mother hasn't got a lot of money so it was all we could afford."

"Oh Hax," said Pho. "Are you sure I can receive these readings for a discount? I will happily pay full price!"

"No, no," said Hax. "I insist!"

Pho smiled. She liked the boy's innocence and friendly nature.

He's too pure for this world, she thought sadly.

Hax opened a side door and ushered Pho inside. In the shack, the smell of scented candles hit the back of Pho's throat, and crystals seemed to hang down from the ceiling. A middle aged lady sat in a large chair with a deck of tarot cards stacked on a small stool before her. She looked up at Pho, and then to Hax.

"This is my friend Pho, mother!" explained Hax proudly.

"Oh, hello my dear," said the woman. "Hax has told me a lot about you! I am Aberdare."

She smiled warmly, and Pho held out her hand in greeting.

"Hax told me you can do psychic readings," Pho explained. "I was wondering if I could get one."

"Of course," she said. "Although I have not done a reading since we moved here. I will be interested to see what the spirits say."

Pho smiled. She was quite a spiritual person, perhaps not on the same level as Aberdare, but she certainly held a keen interest in things such as tarot and certainly star signs – she was a Saggitarius, which in Pho's opinion made a lot of sense as she held a deep love of learning, an adventurous spirit and, despite Luis and her father testing it, was generally quite optimistic.

"Come dear, sit with me," said Aberdare, shuffling her deck of tarot cards.

Pho did as she was told and sat in a chair opposite Hax's mother. Hax sat down a little way off and watched with interest.

"My dear, I can sense immediately that your mind is very troubled," said Aberdare with concern. "There is a man… you are convinced he is not the right one for you. And yet you feel pressure to marry him."

Pho nodded. "And I don't know how to escape from it," she said with sadness.

Aberdare smiled. "But I can also sense your love of shells, dear!" she said. "Especially your prized nautilus shell!"

Pho gasped. She did not think even her father had seen that. All of her shells were special, but her nautilus shell was her favourite. Aberdare's legitimacy had grown.

The lady pulled a card from her tarot deck. Her smile increased.

"I have some good news for you," she announced. "Here I have an Ace of Cups, which tells me there are new beginnings for you on the horizon. A chance to nurture a new idea or pursue new avenues in life. Or perhaps a new romantic interest."

Although Pho felt glad at the optimism, she could not help but feel these were just the ramblings of a mad old woman. She appreciated the sentiment from Aberdare nonetheless. Hax's mother put the card back and slid the deck off to the side. She took Pho's hands in hers.

"I can see you have doubts," she said. "But in order for you to manifest what I have prophesied, you need to have faith and you need to put in the effort to make it a reality. The spirits don't just hand things out for free you know."

Pho nodded in understanding.

"I also sense you carry an object of great significance," said Aberdare unexpectedly.

Pho quickly felt for the glowing gemstone in her robes. She took it out and held it up to Aberdare.

"Hax and I found it in a cave on the beach," she explained. "I… I think it made the lightning try and strike me the other day."

"May I?" asked Aberdare, indicating that she would like to hold it.

Cautiously, Pho handed the woman the sapphire. A look of wonder came across Aberdare's face.

"It is one of the Sajak!" she declared in amazement. "The Sajak are four ancient artefacts that are said to correspond with the Great Spirits of the world of Nearth."

Pho looked in amazement at the glowing jewel. "And we found it in a beach cave?" she asked.

"In the ancient days of the world, the Temple of Nearth sat at the very heart of what is now the Sea of Many Currents. It is said that the last King of Nearth angered the weather spirit, and the spirit flooded the temple, creating the vast blue ocean we now know, separating Xudm from the lands of Harleland far to the north." She smiled. "Perhaps this Sajak was lost in the sea when it first flooded, thousands of years ago, only to eventually be washed ashore."

Aberdare handed the jewel back to Pho.

"Keep it safe Pho, my dear," said Aberdare. "In the wrong hands, a powerful object like this could be used for many evils. However I get the sense that soon, its rightful owner shall come to claim it, and that he will use it for many good things."

"Thank you," said Pho. "Oh, how much will you charge for today's session?"

"Fifty baht, and we'll call–"

CRASH!

Aberdare was cut off as the front door was smashed in. In walked two Belrench officers, and to Pho's horror, they were accompanied by none other than Commander Luis.

"How *dare* you believe yourselves worthy to be in the company of the future wife of a Belrench Commander!" screamed Luis, backing Hax and Aberdare into a corner. Pho was grabbed by the rough hands of one of Luis' officers, and dragged away, while Luis launched into a tirade of ill words to the innocent inhabitants of the house he had just broken into. Pho screamed as she was taken away. She tried to kick at the officer but it was no use.

"Save it, love," he said. "Your fiancé will have some stern words to have with you later, that's for sure."

Somewhere in the back of Pho's mind she swore she heard a voice telling her to use the jewel. How she could use that she had no idea, but she realised with horror that if lightning were to try and strike her again, she would not be opposed to the idea. Eventually she stopped struggling and accepted that she had been caught with Hax red handed. The officer took her closer to her home, where no doubt her father would discipline her. Pho closed her eyes and wept. Aberdare's prophecies seemed a long way from ever coming true.

Chapter Nine

It was a cloudy day when Drew, Josh, Tenebrae and Geetie returned to Boron Nigh. King Lekt demanded they see him immediately, despite Geetie's protests – the jolly man just wanted some time to rest after an exhausting couple of days. Drew's heart bounced in happiness when he entered the Palace of Merthru. That was because, to his surprise, Duchess Wilder sat around the council table, the King at the head, alongside the other Dukes of Harleland.

Drew sneered when he saw Duke Barnshire of Lekt Valley, the unpleasant looking man seeming quite out of place alongside the others. Duke Travis of Cernsland, whom Drew had only seen in passing at a previous council meeting, sat next to Naz, who had been granted Balnather's council seat. On Naz's other side was Duke Ritticüs Czmith of Dirtgula. Ritticüs gave Drew a nod, the events of the journey through Dirtgula clearly being replayed in both of their heads'. One seat remained empty, the one that belonged to the heir to the throne of Harleland. Drew realised with a jolt that Lekt had no heir as of yet. If he were to die, the Lakton Dynasty would end and the next King or Queen would have to be selected from a different family.

"Hail, Andrew Saran!" called the King. He addressed the council: "My friends, today's meeting is at an end. You are all dismissed."

The councillors rose and slowly began to depart. Ritticüs nodded once more as he walked past, stopping to chat with his cousins Geetie and Josh. Drew smiled as he saw Duchess Wilder approach him, while Tenebrae joined Geetie, Josh and Ritticüs. He wondered how things were in Wilder Forest. Although it had been just a week since he had left, it still felt like an age had passed.

"It is good to see you again, Drew," said Wilder.

"Have you survived without me?" asked Drew mischievously.

Wilder laughed. "Oh, no, barely surviving," she said sarcastically. "I hoped to see you when we first arrived yesterday, but King Lekt said you had gone on another quest."

"I do that a lot," replied Drew. "I'm surprised you travelled here for a council meeting. Have you been able to talk things over with Lekt yet?"

Wilder shook her head. "I came because it's my duty to my people. I have not spoken privately with Lekt." She sighed. "Not since last year."

Drew looked at her in sadness. "I think you should put your animosity aside," he suggested. "For the good of both Wilder Forest and Harleland."

"General Sylvia tells me the same," she admitted. "A wise leader listens to the advice of her Generals, and her friends." She sighed. "Perhaps I'm not as wise as my foremothers."

Drew looked at her reassuringly.

"You are very wise," replied Drew. "And I think you know deep down that the right thing to do is speak with Lekt and air your grievances."

Wilder smiled. "Thanks, Drew," she said. "I will consider it."

Ritticüs departed, and Geetie, Josh and Tenebrae joined the King at the council table.

"Andrew!" called Lekt. "We must speak, my friend!"

Drew took his leave and walked over to where Lekt and Chief Naz waited. Geetie, Josh and Tenebrae already sat on chairs around the council table in the middle of the great hall. The King invited Drew to sit.

"Josh has told us of your meeting with Kora the Dragon," Lekt began.

Naz's eyes lit up. "How is she?" he asked. "You found her cave with no problems?"

"Eventually," laughed Tenebrae.

"I had to use the runes to find the entrance," admitted Drew. "It was hidden."

"I suppose that Horath was able to use her magic to open the entrance for us," admitted Naz, referring to the Witch of Cold Valley. "I never realised it was usually hidden."

"We were given a cryptic message by Kora," said Drew.

He repeated the strange prophecy once more.

Across a blue ocean, with many flows,

To Xudm's lands, an evil grows,

A child keeps the Ocean Sapphire,

But to end the dark, one must know,

Defeat the evil, and another will grow.

"Xudm?" said Lekt in surprise. "Well that is only a small land, although it lies directly south over the Sea of Many Currents." He paused. "It is a client Kingdom of Belrance. King Benjamin the Great owns it."

"Well 'blue ocean, with many flows' clearly refers to the Sea of Many Currents," said Tenebrae thoughtfully.

"Could we send messengers to King Ben?" suggested Naz. "Perhaps he could help us search Xudm for the sapphire."

"Nay," said Lekt. "I haven't met Ben, but I know that he and my father had a rocky relationship. I have a feeling that if he knew the Ocean Sapphire was in one of his client Kingdoms, he would jump at the chance to claim that jewel for himself."

"Tell me more about Xudm," requested Drew. "It's a client Kingdom you say?"

"It was colonised by Belrance many years ago," explained Naz.

"And a good thing too!" said Lekt. "The Belrench have improved the living standards of Xudists tenfold since they arrived."

Drew narrowed his eyes. There was certainly a reason why Duchess Wilder did not get along with the King. Looking around the table, he could tell the others were in agreement.

"Uh," began Naz, breaking the awkward silence. "If King Ben won't help us, the only other thing I can suggest is a covert mission to Xudm." He looked at Drew and Josh. "I am sure our stand out Protectors here would be up for the mission."

"Hey!" called Tenebrae. "You ain't leaving me out!"

"Yeah!" said Geetie. "Octavia is our friend too. We want to help save him."

Drew felt warmth flow through him at his friends opting to join.

"So be it," declared Naz. "I shall arrange for a ship to be prepared for you, by the Port of Boron Nigh." He paused. "Be warned though. The Sea of Many Currents has that name for a reason. The currents are treacherous, and the sea storms are legendary."

"We've faced sea storms before," Josh pointed out. "When we crossed the Sea of the Sun to Wiln!"

"And I grew up in the isles of the Outer Dirtgulas!" boasted Geetie. "I've sailed the Sea of the Sun and the Great Southern Sea!" But then the food merchant had a serious look come over his face. "But I know the reputation of the Sea of Many Currents."

Naz nodded. "It is more dangerous than the Sea of the Sun. You can be sure of that."

The Sea of Many Currents existed to the west of the Great Southern Sea, and lay between Harleland's south-west coast and Xudm's north coast. Naz explained that it was a week's journey to cross to the other side. That also factored in the expected bad weather and difficult currents. It did not factor in any unexpectedly large sea storms.

"It seems, my friends, that you will all need your wits about you," said Lekt.

"Indeed," continued Geetie. "But our friend is in danger, and I'm willing to risk my life for him."

Tenebrae nodded. "I agree," she said.

Drew looked at Geetie and Tenebrae in pride. How he had been lucky enough to find friends like them, he had no idea.

"I think we should set out first thing tomorrow morning!" suggested Josh.

"Ah, to hell with all these early starts," complained Geetie. "Can't a man sleep in?"

They all laughed. But then, Lekt looked at them all seriously.

"However, the last two lines of the prophecy," he said. "About a new evil growing. Just be careful out there."

"Do you think it refers to this *him* that Octavia was talking about?" asked Tenebrae.

Drew nodded. "Perhaps," he said. "It means at the very least that somewhere in Xudm, a hidden danger lurks."

***

Later that day, Naz sent his messengers to the port. The company retired to their assigned quarters for the night. As they left, Drew exchanged a quick glance of farewell with Duchess Wilder. He wondered when they would see each other again? He had grown fond of her, and the unorthodox way of life she and her people in Wilder Forest lived. They waved at each other as Drew turned into the dormitory.

In the quarters, Geetie took out his Lyre and began to play a tune. The food merchant claimed the words had come to him earlier over dinner, as he had pondered the upcoming journey over the sea.

"*Ohhhh–*

The sea swirls, and the wind roars!

Under a stormy sky and battlin' the mighty oars!

We'll hoist the sail, despite the hail!"

Tenebrae and Josh joined in the tune, while Drew sat silently. His mind was elsewhere, taken up by anxieties over Octavia, the Weather Runes, the Ocean Sapphire and whatever these evils they had to face were. One would fall and another would rise. It made Drew feel sick.

"Come on Drew, join in!" called Tenebrae.

"*But at the captain's shout, "Brace the mast!"*

And then a flash of light, as the storm causes fright!

But if we fight the night, we will be all... right!"

Drew smiled. The song began to ease his thoughts, and soon he joined in with the others. His resolve hardened. Octavia was counting on him. Perhaps, with the Weather Runes at stake, so was the entire Kingdom. But he also knew Octavia well. The old man would not be happy if Drew was missing out on enjoying himself on his account. But then, a dark thought penetrated his mind. What would happen if this supposed threat found the Ocean Sapphire first? Or if Octavia's condition worsened? What would happen if Drew and his friends were too late?

Chapter Ten

Pho sighed as she picked up the mop. She had been ordered
to clean the floors of the kitchen today, after being made
yesterday to clean debris from the yard. Yes, these chores
were a punishment. Usually, her father would deal with the
yard, while Pho helped her mother with tasks inside the
house. But since Luis had caught her at Hax's house, Pho
had been made to take on all household chores for the next
month. Her father had been livid, as expected. She shivered
as she remembered the force of his hand coming into contact
with her cheek after Luis' officer had dragged her home. She
was not allowed to leave the house under any circumstances,
unless Luis accompanied her.

He was also very disappointed. The Commander had gone
on and on about how 'disrespectful' Pho had been towards
him, and had complained about how 'trouble makers' such
as Hax should have no place in society. Speaking of Hax –
he and his mother had been given orders to leave Phārā. Pho
was not permitted to say goodbye, and for all she knew, her
only friend was now miles away in another village. Not for
the first time, a tear rolled down her face. She hated this. She
hated her father. She hated Luis. And she hated herself for
seemingly being unable to help herself. After she had
completed her mopping, Pho threw herself down on a chair
in the living room. She took out the glowing jewel. Perhaps
this weird stone was the only hope she had left. If, as
Aberdare had said, it was one of the so-called Sajak, perhaps
she could find some way to use it. Was it like a genie?
Perhaps it could grant her three wishes. What would she
wish for first?

"I wish for Luis to just go away and leave me alone," she said, holding the jewel to her mouth.

Nothing happened, and the sapphire continued to glow blue as it had always done. Perhaps it did not have the power to grant wishes. Pho sighed. The only thing this stupid rock *had* done was try and strike her with lightning. Maybe that was what it did. Controlled the weather. Or something. Pho rolled her eyes at how stupid that sounded. She wandered over the window and looked out at the grey skies. A slight drizzle was falling, reflecting her sombre mood. Perhaps she should just give up and marry Luis tomorrow. The thought of being with the man made her sick to her stomach, but at this point, what other choice did she have?

***

"There was good fishing today, Pho!" said Chip, as he chowed down on some cod. "Mara and I caught a load! Two cod and three bluefin tuna! Enough for the next week at least!"

Pho smiled at her father. He seemed to have calmed down over the past day and was actually talking to her like his daughter again. She still felt resentment towards him, however she felt relief at his friendlier mood.

"Would you like some more beans, dear?" asked her mother.

"Yes please," replied Pho.

This was the first family dinner they had had since she had been grounded, and despite her feeling awkward sitting with her parents, a warm feeling of belonging came back over her.

"So," began Chip. He seemed to consider his next words carefully. "Your mother and I have been thinking. It's come to our attention that you, perhaps, aren't the biggest fan of Commander Luis."

Pho had to stop herself from saying 'obviously.' She held her tongue and continued to listen to her father.

"Luis and I had a talk today… we think perhaps it is best for you two to take a break from each other for at least the rest of the month."

Some weird feeling – was it a feeling of freedom? – shot through Pho.

"Oh, yes," she said. "That would be great."

"Excellent!" declared Chip. "A break will do you both good. And hopefully by the end, you shall both realise how much you miss each other."

Pho stopped herself from scowling. But this was an opportunity. All she had to do was use the next few weeks to try and convince her father that it would be better for her to *not* be with Luis at all.

"Oh, father?" began Pho. "Am I still grounded?"

Chip sighed. "I'm afraid so," he said. "What you did in defying your husband-to-be was disrespectful, and as I am responsible for you until you are married to Luis, I must ensure that I am being seen as a responsible father."

Pho's resentment returned. She pushed her plate away, her half-eaten beans not looking as appetizing as they were a few minutes ago.

"You're finished already?" asked her mother.

"Yes, I'm not exactly that hungry anymore," said Pho.

"Make sure you come down and wash up later," commanded her father. "Remember, you're still grounded."

Pho retreated upstairs to her room, her fists clenched. She squeezed them so tightly together that her knuckles began to appear white. This man just did not understand. He was so out of touch, it appeared impossible to ever convince him of freeing her from marrying Luis. Pho closed the door and threw herself down onto her bed and cried. There was no way out. She was trapped. Her father on one hand, and Luis on the other, working together it seemed to make her life miserable. The rain outside began to pour heavily now, clanging down upon the wooden roof. She jumped as she heard the sound of thunder in the distance. The last time there had been a storm was the day she nearly got struck by lightning. Pho rolled over onto her back, the dim candle light in her room reflecting off her tear streaked face. She pulled out the gemstone again. She gazed at it in wonder. It seemed to be pulsating with energy, in a way she had not seen it do before. Suddenly, a voice spoke to her.

You have a Sajak, it said, causing Pho to jump in shock. *You have ascended beyond Luis now! Use it…*

Pho threw the jewel at her doorway. Almost instantly, the pulsating power from the sapphire seemed to cease. She got up quietly, the sound of rain having also stopped. Pho tip toed over to the stone and looked at it.

"Did you just... speak to me?" she asked.

No response. She picked up the stone. She decided to ask it again, now that it was in her hand.

"Did you just speak?" she asked, more confidently.

It depends on who you mean by 'you,' replied the voice.

Pho gasped. "Who are you?" she asked. "If not this Sajak thing?"

I am lots of things, Pho my dear, replied the voice. *Perhaps I am this stone. Perhaps I am something... more.*

Pho shook her head. Something about this voice seemed... off putting. Like it had ill intentions. She put the stone down on her bedside table.

And now I've just gone and summoned an evil spirit! she thought with despair. As if things could get any worse!

Then she froze. The light of her candle dimmed. A horrible, cold feeling washed over her. There was someone – or something – in the room with her. Pho dared not turn around. The hairs on the back of her neck stood up. Whatever this entity was was standing right behind her. Pho closed her eyes. She began breathing heavily. Tears began to form in her closed eyes. And then at that moment the door opened, and in walked her father.

"Pho!" he called. "It's time for you to clean the dishes."

Pho opened her eyes and turned around. Whatever entity had appeared in her room was gone, and the candle light returned to its former strength.

"Yes, father," she stammered. "I'm coming."

"Are you okay?" he asked with concern. "It's not something I said earlier, right?"

Pho shook her head. "No, it's… it's nothing. I'll be down."

Her father nodded and walked out. Pho knew what she had to do. This Sajak thing was trouble and needed to go. She grabbed the sapphire and put it back into her robes, before proceeding to descend the stairs to attend to her chores.

Tonight, she thought. *Tonight, I'll sneak out and bury this thing. So that this evil spirit, or whatever it is, can never harm anyone!*

Of course, my dear, the voice replied. *I'd like to see you try.*

Chapter Eleven

Drew stood at the dock, gazing out over the vast, endless water. To his left were the great sea cliffs that marked the meeting point between the Dirtgula Mountains and the sea. To his right, the land thinned out into a beach, a headland sitting at the end. Beyond that headland was another beach, followed by another headland, and so on, and so forth. The Port of Boron Nigh stood where the cliffs of the Dirtgula Mountains dropped into the sea, at the edge of Harleland's southwest coast – where the vast Great Southern Sea gave way to the swirling Sea of Many Currents, which stretched for supposedly a tick over nine hundred kilometers and separated Harleland from Xudm, their destination.

"Drew," said a familiar voice.

Drew turned and saw Jemima, Naz's partner, and recently promoted harbourmaster of the Port of Boron Nigh.

"The ship is prepared," she explained.

"Jemima!" said Drew. "It is good to see you again. How are you and Naz? He said that you have moved together to the port here?"

Jemima nodded. "Yes, we found a nice seaside cottage to settle in together," she said. "Things are going well! Did he tell you? We're to be married in the Spring!"

"Oh, congratulations!" said Drew. "I'm sure there will be a big wedding planned? After all, the Chief of the Protectors marrying the harbourmaster is quite a big news story."

"Well, we try and keep it a bit quiet," Jemima said sheepishly. "We'd rather not have those pesky scribes and inkmen writing about us in the city sheets."

Drew laughed. "No, of course not," he said. "But come on, show me the ship!"

Jemima led Drew down the dock and toward a large looking boat. Smaller than a warship, that was for sure, but large enough that it could cut through the fierce waves of the Sea of Many Currents.

"Wow!" said the voice of Geetie, as he approached the pair. "This beauty is certainly bigger than *The Sea Sprinter* back in the Port of Dirtgula!"

Drew smiled as he remembered the old battered merchant boat that the Dirtgulans had lent them to cross the Sea of the Sun to Wiln on the quest to the Great Tower. This ship was much bigger and mightier.

"This is *The Ocean Herald*," explained Jemima. "It's generally used as a patrol boat by the Navy, but it hasn't been deployed since before the Uprising movement took over."

"Shall I fetch the others?" asked Geetie. "I'll get Josh and Tenebrae to start loading the ship!"

"Well, the ship is yours," said Jemima. "But you'll be staying a night here, surely?"

Drew's heart felt hollow. "I wish we could but… we've delayed long enough already. Who knows how long Octavia has left."

"A shame," said Jemima. "Lilthyme and Kulu are stationed here now too, and they'd have loved to see you."

"And what about the other Protectors who were exiled to Cold Valley?" asked Geetie.

Jemima thought for a moment. "Reke has retired and gone to live with his wife and children in Cernsland," she explained. "Ketlaz has been stationed near Canterbury, on the Greenarch Plain. Oh, and Jerzuan left the Protectors to open a nice little shop in Hogs!" Her expression darkened. "And of course, former Sergeant Elias was tried for treason, and remains imprisoned to this day."

"Elias got what he deserved then," said Geetie with a scowl. "After what that traitor did."

Drew had barely met Elias, and had only briefly met with most of the Protectors who had been exiled with Naz and Jemima in Cold Valley, but he knew that Geetie had developed a soft spot for them all after the food merchant went searching for them, and later joined them in the Revolt of Boron Nigh.

"I shall have to visit Jerzuan's shop next time I go to Hogs!" declared Geetie. "I'm sure I could hook him up with some good business connections!"

Drew felt impatience course through him. It was already midday, and he wanted to be away as soon as possible.

"Maybe I'll go help Josh and Tenebrae with loading the ship," he said.

"Oh, very well!" said Geetie. "Well Jemima, let's have a little catch up, shall we?"

Drew felt bad for not staying and talking with Jemima, but there were more pressing matters at hand. He walked toward the storage hut where he knew Josh and Tenebrae were preparing food, clothes and weapons for their sea crossing. As he entered the hut, he saw Tenebrae making a fuss over some old maps.

"…and if we get the navigation wrong, we could end up stranded on some island!" she was saying as Drew walked in.

"Islands?" asked Drew.

"Apparently there are a few small uninhabited islands closer to Xudm," explained Josh. "Tenebrae seems to think we'll hit them if we don't choose the right map."

"There are four charts here, and none of them agree on where the currents run or where the islands even are!" said Tenebrae exasperated. "How can Geetie navigate us if there's different maps saying different things?"

"I'm sure Geetie is experienced enough with sea navigation to know what he's doing," said Drew. "Don't panic, Tenebrae."

"I wasn't panicking!" said Tenebrae defensively. Then she sighed. "Okay, I guess I'm a bit nervous about going to sea again after what happened last time."

Drew understood. A powerful wave had crashed over them as they sailed to Wiln, causing them to be washed up on the shore of the isle of Grashnâk. They were lucky then that Geetie's grandmother, Ern, lived on the island and helped them to recover. Ern's Tribemates even helped rebuild their vessel so they could set off again and complete the crossing to Wiln. But this time, with no inhabited island between Harleland and Xudm, there would be no help for them if they washed ashore. The other difference this time around was the lack of Octavia. At that time, he had been the Chief of the Protectors, and he led the company with a confidence that only Octavia could channel. This time though, the now retired Chief lay dying in a hospital bed somewhere in Boron Nigh, that fact being the main reason for this quest in the first place.

And the Weather Runes, thought Drew, remembering that the Ocean Sapphire was made of the next five runes he was meant to collect and master.

Drew suddenly remembered something else. Something he had not heard in the year since he had obtained the Life Runes from the Green Tree. For a time, he had been haunted by a strange voice that whispered dark secrets and encouraged him to commit violent deeds. Shortly after he had used the Life Rune *Protect* to summon a giant shield to surround Boron Nigh, protecting it from the Herk battalion of the Crownlands, the voice of Lazarka, the Demi-god of Life, had freed him of the evil entity. He had not heard from the dark voice – or from Lazarka – since that day. Still, part of him wondered: where had it gone? And would it ever return?

After a few more minutes, Drew, Josh and Tenebrae had successfully loaded *The Ocean Herald* with all the supplies that they would need for the journey. The trio, as well as Geetie, climbed aboard the ship, and turned to face Jemima back on the dock, who had been joined by Naz, Lilthyme and Kulu.

"You're sure you won't stay just one night?" pleaded Naz.

"I'm itching to go," said Drew. "When we return, and Octavia is healed, I promise to you that we'll all celebrate with a night to remember."

"We'll hold you to that!" called Jemima mischievously.

"Count me in!" said Geetie in excitement.

"Farewell!" called Lilthyme, as the rope tying the ship to the dock was undone.

"Good luck!" echoed Kulu, *The Ocean Herald* now beginning to float away.

Drew smiled at his fellow Protectors and then turned to face the direction of travel. His heart sank at the sight. Blue, rolling waves, as far as the eye could see.

"Big day tomorrow," he murmured to himself sadly, the memory of Octavia washing over him. "More sea…"

He laughed as he remembered Octavia's sarcasm as they crossed the Sea of the Sun to Wiln. Drew knew that he was more than capable of leading missions without Octavia now. After all, Octavia had not been present when he, Josh and Tenebrae went to Wilder Forest to look for the then-Prince Lekt. But as Drew looked at the Naval vessel he and the others now sailed upon, the weight of his responsibilities began to hang heavy on him.

"Cheer up, Drew!" said Josh, patting his master on the back. "In a few days we'll have landed in Xudm, and then a few days after that we'll have the Ocean Sapphire, ready to cross the sea back home!"

"I wish it seemed that simple," said Drew sadly. "But I have the feeling it won't be all smooth sailing."

"I get it!" called Geetie. "Smooth sailing! 'Cause we're on a boat! Ha!"

Josh rolled his eyes, while Drew put his head in his hand.

"And you could have someone big and serious like King Lekt with you!" said Geetie, eyeing the pair crossly. "Instead you have a light hearted moron like me! Count your blessings." He smiled, laughed, and returned to the captain's bridge, whistling.

Drew laughed himself, and that caused Josh to break out in a smile. "We *are* lucky to have your father," admitted Drew.

"We are," replied Josh. "We really, truly are."

So it was that *The Ocean Herald* sailed at a good speed toward the horizon. By the time the sun began to set, Harleland was no longer visible in the direction they had come, the company now surrounded on all sides by what felt like an endless expanse of ocean, sky and destiny. The quest for the Ocean Sapphire had truly begun.

Chapter Twelve

It was midnight. Pho made sure that her parents were both asleep before slipping out of her room, sneaking down the stairs and quietly leaving the house. In her robes was the Sajak, this strange object that had first tried to kill her, and was now trying to haunt her. But no more. Tonight, she was going down to the beach to bury this horrible thing before it could do anymore damage. She was taking a risk no matter what she did – if she was caught by her parents, or god forbid by Luis – who could say what her next punishment would be. Yet if she did not get rid of this jewel, then who could say what evil spirits would come after her next. She shuddered as she remembered the awful cold feeling of whatever creature stood behind her in her bedroom earlier that evening.

Pho made her way quietly through the village and towards the beach. Adrenaline pumped through her veins. She relished the feeling of being outside once more, and the thought of being back on the beach made her feel alive. Those feelings were multiplied when Pho finally stepped out onto the shore. The waves crashed against the sandy beach, and stars glittered through the scattered clouds above. The rain earlier in the evening had all but vanished, and now the night was cool and crisp. Pho ran down to the water's edge and got down on her knees. She had decided that she would bury the gemstone below the watermark, so that it could be washed out to sea eventually. She deduced that throwing it out to sea would result in it being washed ashore once more, and she did not want to ever see this awful artefact ever again. She began digging, her hands becoming caked in sand as she dug deeper and deeper. Her knees and lower legs became soaked by the endless waves that lapped at her. Finally, after several minutes, Pho was happy with the hole she had dug and proceeded to plant the glowing stone at the bottom. She began to fill it back in, burying the gemstone for good. She stood and watched with satisfaction as a wave came by to smooth out the area she had buried the rock in.

Pho gave a sigh of relief. That was one problem dealt with. She made her way back up the beach towards the village, scrapping sand off of her as she silently passed through the town's alleys, before getting back to her front door. Once she was up the stairs and had her bedroom door closed, she threw herself to the floor and allowed herself to celebrate. For the next hour or more, Pho cleaned herself, removing all evidence that she had been to the beach, before finally climbing into bed and falling to sleep.

***

"…yes, I know dear! Wait. Pho! Come see!"

Pho was awoken by her mother barging into her room.

"You'll never believe what your father found on the beach this morning!" she exclaimed.

Pho sat bolt upright. No. It could not be the jewel. Surely her mother referred to something else. She cautiously rose from the bed and followed her mother downstairs. Sure enough, to Pho's utter dismay, her father stood with Commander Luis in the living room, holding the glowing blue gemstone in his hand.

"I have never seen anything like it!" her father exclaimed. "But there it was, on the beach as I did my morning walk! Ha!"

"Usually such an object is reserved only for the Royals of Belrance," explained Luis, clearly ogling Pho as she stood in her nightgown. "But I hope that perhaps it can be used as yet another mark of our enduring love."

Luis took the stone from Chip and handed it to Pho.

"I know, my love, that your father and I decided on a small break from each other, but… This jewel here is far too beautiful to not give you as a gift."

Pho felt sick as Luis placed the stone in her hand. He stepped back with her father.

"When we rekindle our love in a few weeks, I hope that this gift shall finally sway you that we are meant to be!" sung Luis. "Until then, farewell."

He promptly left the house, with Chip and Thu staring at the jewel in awe.

"No greater gift could be given!" said Chip. "For a Belrench Commander to allow us to keep such an exquisite object!"

Pho hated the way in which Luis had gifted her the jewel. Her *father* had found it, not him, yet the Commander seemed to act as if it was his property, purely because of his membership of the Belrench race.

"It wasn't his to give," said Pho.

"It is on Belrench soil," replied her father. "You should be grateful to him!"

Defeated, Pho took the gemstone back upstairs to her room. She closed the door and sat upon her bed, staring at it.

"You win," she mumbled.

She swore she heard faint, jeering laughter in her head, but other than that, there was no response from the mysterious voice. Her frustrations grew when she heard her father knocking on the door.

"Pho, come down and help your mother with breakfast!" he called.

Annoyed, she changed into a robe, slipped the stone inside its inner pocket, and returned downstairs to help Thu. Her mother slaved away over a hot frying pan, bacon sizzling on the fine metal surface, while eggs boiled in a pot.

Pho grabbed a loaf of bread and began slicing it. Her mother looked at her happily as she piled the bacon onto three separate plates.

"I know your father can be a nuisance sometimes," said Thu. "And yes, I admit he sometimes puts the status of our family before you. But he does it because he genuinely believes that increased status will benefit you in the long-term."

"I understand that," replied Pho. "It's just that I believe I should get a choice. My sister got a choice, my brother got a choice – why not me?"

Thu sighed. "Your father will always regret letting your brother move to the Augustan Empire," she said. "And your sister was married and moved to Mạttā before Luis was posted here. He sees you as the family's last chance to gain status."

"I just want to live," admitted Pho. "I don't care about status. I just want to live…"

Pho and Thu served up breakfast, Chip coming to join them for another family meal.

"Thanks for helping cook, Pho," said Chip warmly, clearly trying to present himself as caring.

Pho was not having it, and she just smiled awkwardly at him, before beginning to eat. The family ate in silence, and soon enough, Pho was back in the kitchen cleaning the dishes. And that was when the thoughts began circulating in her head – the thoughts of running away.

***

For the rest of the day, Pho sat in her room, thinking. She gave thought to the blue jewel in her robes. How was it that her father of all people had found it on the beach? Was this thing powerful enough that it could make its way back to her if it wanted to? The other thing that was on her mind was her sister. Her name was Ara, and Pho had not seen her since she visited last year. She smiled at the thought of seeing her again. Mạttā was a two day ride from Phārā, and despite their family's close ties with Commander Luis, they had no horses. This meant that whenever the family came together,

they would have to fork out thousands of baht for a horse
and carriage hire.

But Pho was formulating an idea. A bold one. One where
there would be no going back. What would happen if she ran
away? She could run all the way to Mąttā and live with her
sister. She always remembered when her and Ara had
fantasised about coming to see each other multiple times per
year once they were both married. Of course reality meant
that it was unaffordable, and Pho as a single woman would
never be allowed to travel to Mąttā by herself. But if she ran
away then there would be no way for anyone to enforce that
rule. Pho looked at the blue jewel.

"What should I do?" she asked.

Run, the voice replied. *Run and be free!*

Resolve hardened within Pho. She would run. She would be
free. She felt sadness course through her as she stared around
her room. She had made this place her own over her entire
life, and she knew she would be unable to return. Her shell
collection, her artwork she had stuck on the walls... A tear
fell. She could either stay trapped in her homely prison or
flee to a life of freedom with her sister. She knew what to do.
She spent the rest of the afternoon assembling a small pack
of essentials and looking over her shell collection one last
time. Tonight, she would leave. Tonight, Pho would run
away.

Chapter Thirteen

The ship swayed in the breeze as Drew helped Josh to rig the sail. Geetie stood at the wheel, while Tenebrae had retreated into the cabin with sea sickness.

"Pull!" called Geetie above the rising wind.

Drew did as commanded and the sail was hoisted higher, taking advantage of the greater wind that was blowing from a north-easterly direction.

"Prepare to tack!" called Geetie again, as Drew and Josh held onto a nearby railing. With a jolt, the ship turned sharply and surged forward at speed. The rockiness subsided as *The Ocean Herald* cut through the waves like a high quality knife. Drew sighed with relief, while Josh sat himself down on a stool next to the mast.

"What would we do without Captain Geetie?" asked Drew in amusement.

"I'm sure if he had his way, he'd sail the seven seas for eternity," replied Josh.

Drew laughed. "Anyways, I'd better go check on Tenebrae. She didn't look too well."

Josh nodded, and Drew went inside the cabin. It was nice to have an indoor quarters aboard this vessel, unlike the small merchant boat they had sailed from Dirtgula to Wiln fourteen months prior. The cabin was surprisingly cosy, a small fire burning in the hearth on the far wall, while a comfy queen bed sat off to the side, and a dining table graced the middle of the room.

Drew, Josh and Geetie had set up hammocks on the wall opposite the bed, with Tenebrae's sea sickness allowing her to sleep in luxury.

"Are you okay?" asked Drew, looking upon her pale face.

"I will be," said Tenebrae. "I'm better than I was twenty minutes ago."

"You'll get used to the sea," said Drew. "Trust me, in the next day or so you'll be back in tip top shape!"

"I hope so," said Tenebrae. "I feel trapped. Like all I want is to lie down on solid, dry land… but I can't."

"This cabin is as dry as it will get for now I'm afraid," said Drew. He did not know how to comfort Tenebrae, and he was unsure if he even wanted to try. Her volatile nature often meant she misconstrued help as thinking she was weak.

"If you need anything, let me know," said Drew tactfully.

"Thanks, Drew," answered Tenebrae.

Drew left the cabin and returned to the deck. He decided to climb up to the captain's deck and speak to Geetie about their progress.

"We've come a long way, actually," said Geetie. "I deduce by the way the currents run that we have travelled four thousand chains from the Port of Boron Nigh."

"It's nine hundred kilometers to the coast of Xudm, right?" asked Drew.

"Approximately, yes," replied Geetie. "We still haven't come up with a story for if we're intercepted by the Belrench Navy," he pointed out.

Drew nodded. "I've been thinking about that. What if we told them that King Lekt wishes to introduce himself to the Lord of Xudm? Lekt *is* still relatively new, and it's certainly a passable excuse."

Geetie nodded. "That could work," he said. "Well, at least we don't have to worry about Herks this time… Ho, sailor!" he called to Josh on the deck below. "Come! We must discuss tactics!"

Josh ascended the ladder and joined Drew and Geetie by the wheel.

"After all," continued Geetie. "You two are the Protectors here, not me."

Drew smiled. "In another life, you would have made a fine Protector," he said.

Geetie shook his head. "I still haven't gotten over killing Count Mossjoint during the Revolt of Boron Nigh," he said.

Drew realised with a jolt that tears had begun to well up in the food merchant's eyes. Mossjoint, despite being one of the Inquisitors of the corrupt Uprising movement, was Geetie's first and only kill, and it would be a deed that would haunt the usually jolly man for the rest of his days.

Geetie shook himself. "So… No, a Protector's life is not for me," he said. "But I shall always assist the *good* Protectors such as you two, and Naz of course, wherever possible."

Drew smiled at the man, and then turned to Josh. He told his apprentice of the idea to tell the Belrench that they were seeking to treat with the Lord of Xudm should they be questioned.

Josh nodded in agreement. "It sounds like a common sense plan," he said. "But how much control over Xudm does Belrance have? I know Xudm is a client Kingdom, and it is owned by Belrance, but what happens if the Belrench Navy force us to treat with King Ben instead?"

Drew felt anxiety course through him. The very idea of being forced off course to mainland Belrance to visit King Benjamin the Great instead of Xudm made him feel sick. Octavia would die for sure, and whoever this evil individual who sought the runes was would surely get the Ocean Sapphire.

"It's the only way," said Drew. "We're entering Belrench waters. We just have to hope that they will allow us to enter Xudm."

Drew looked out across the endless water, anxiety gnawing at his stomach. Then, without another word, he turned and descended from the bridge and went back inside the cabin. He saw Tenebrae sitting up, alert. Was something wrong?

"Are you okay?" he asked.

"I'm hearing noises," said Tenebrae. "It's like there's something below deck."

Drew shrugged. "It's probably just rats. Or a cat. Most of these ships have a cat aboard to deal with the rodents."

"Maybe," replied Tenebrae. "But it's still giving me the creeps."

"If it makes you feel any better, Josh and I can go down there and investigate," he offered.

"I could investigate myself!" said Tenebrae, a touch testily. "If I wasn't sick."

"I know, I know," said Drew. He sighed. Sometimes he felt like he was walking on eggshells around Tenebrae when it came to offering help.

"But you are sick," he continued. "Please let Josh and I investigate."

"Okay," said Tenebrae. "It's just, it makes me feel useless laying here like this, doing nothing." She sighed. "It goes against who I am."

"I know," said Drew soothingly. "But we're all friends. We should all *expect* each other to help one another. Trust me – Josh and I think you're anything *but* weak."

Tenebrae smiled. "Thanks, Drew," she said.

With that, Drew fetched Josh and the duo opened one of the grates on the floor of the deck.

"Must be big rodents for Tenebrae to hear anything," warned Josh. "I'd be prepared for anything. Just in case."

"Good sentiment," said Drew. "And I'm always prepared." He winked.

The duo jumped down below the deck. Drew lit a candle and looked around. Some bunk beds for a small crew could be seen surrounding them, as well as some small tables which had surely, in Drew's mind, seen many a game of cards or liar's dice. In a far corner, barrels were stacked up. Some seemed to be full of armour, some seemed to be half full of rum, and others were empty.

"Well, drinks tonight?" asked Drew with pleasure at seeing the alcohol.

"Don't tell my father," answered Josh.

Suddenly, there was a clang. Drew and Josh whipped around and saw a shield had dropped on the ground. It wobbled around for a few seconds, the metal echoing against the wooden floor, before settling.

"Who's there?" called Drew. He felt the hairs on his neck prick up. They were being watched. Did they have stowaways? "Show yourself! You can't hide."

Josh unsheathed his blade, while Drew put his hand on his sword's handle. Suddenly, a figure came out from behind some barrels on the other side of the room with his hands raised. He was followed by two more, who also raised their hands. As Drew's shock subsided and his vision adjusted to the gloom, he noticed the glint of familiar armour – dark and weather-worn. Herk armour. Recognition hit him like a wave.

"Oh no…" whispered Josh.

It was Captain Crysthan, Irk and Murk.

Chapter Fourteen

It was a cool evening when Pho slipped quietly out of her parents' front door. Her small pack weighed heavy on her as she made for the main road out of Phārā. She felt intimidated by the multi-day walk to Mạttā, but she felt even more intimidated by the prospect of being forcibly married off to Commander Luis and losing all of the freedoms she craved.

Before she knew it, Pho had left the village behind and walked now along the road, the Northern Jungle of Xudm growing on each side of the path. In her right hand she held an old map of Xudm, and once more she opened it to ensure she was following the right path.

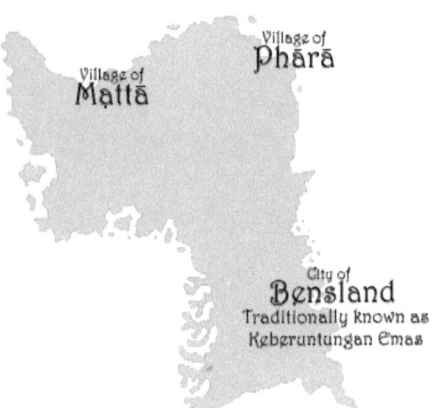

Belreneh Client Kingdom of
Xudm

Village of
Phārā

Village of
Mạttā

City of
Bensland
Traditionally known as
Keberuntungan Emas

Although many villages dotted the land, this map – drawn by her village's cartographer – had been made specifically for her parents to use on visits to Mạttā to see her sister. She cringed as she looked down the dark road. She knew that it was unsafe for a girl of her age to be wandering the roads outside of a village at night. Bandits were known to roam in these rural areas, and she would have a big red target right on her back.

Pho walked on tentatively, jumping at even the slightest sound of a leaf falling or a bat screeching. At some point, she had decided to stick closer to the side of the road where she was less easily seen, lest she be spotted by people with bad intentions. After about two hours, and with the moon now beginning to set in the dark early morning sky, she began to regret her decision to run away. She was cold and terrified, and she felt at every step that she would be accosted by bandits.

Pho's heart raced as she paused to catch her breath. The rustling of the wind in the trees seemed to mimic hurried whispers, and every shadow looked like a figure ready to pounce. The weight of her small pack pressed into her shoulders, grounding her momentarily. She tightened her grip on the map, the coarse paper offering a strange sense of comfort.

"No turning back," she whispered, voice trembling.

Her parents would be furious, and Commander Luis... she shuddered at the thought. No, returning was not an option.

Determined to press on, Pho scanned the path ahead. The road stretched long and lonely, its surface dimly illuminated by the sliver of moonlight peeking through the clouds. A small copse of trees loomed nearby, their gnarled branches beckoning like the twisted fingers of old storytellers. Pho debated seeking refuge there until dawn, but the idea of being surrounded by darkness without even the semblance of a path was more frightening than the open road.

As she trudged forward, her thoughts drifted to Maṭṭā. Her sister Ara's letters had painted a picture of a bustling town with warm hearts and kind faces. It was her beacon of hope, a place where she could find safety and freedom. Pho clung to that vision, letting it propel her weary legs onward.

Then she heard it – the unmistakable sound of footsteps behind her. They were faint at first, but steadily grew louder. Her breath caught in her throat. Pho froze, her mind racing. Could it be a traveler? A bandit? Or worse?

She glanced over her shoulder but saw nothing in the murky distance. The footsteps stopped. Her pulse thundered in her ears as she forced herself to move again, her pace quickening. She clutched her pack tightly, her free hand brushing the small knife she'd taken from the kitchen before leaving.

She dared not to speak and chose to pretend the footsteps were not real. Perhaps it was the Sajak jewel playing tricks on her.

Suddenly, a figure emerged from the shadows ahead, stepping into the faint glow of the moonlight. Pho's stomach dropped. It was a man, tall and broad-shouldered, wearing a cloak that obscured his features. He stood still, as if waiting for her to make the next move.

"Who's there?" she called out, trying to sound braver than she felt. The silence that followed was deafening.

Pho's instincts screamed at her to run, but her legs felt like lead. The man raised a hand, palm open in what she hoped was a gesture of peace.

"Easy now," he said, his voice calm but firm. "I mean you no harm. Are you lost, girl?"

Pho hesitated, her fingers curling tighter around the knife hilt. She couldn't discern his intentions, but there was something unsettling about how he'd appeared so suddenly.

"I… I'm fine," she managed to stammer, taking a cautious step back. "Just passing through."

The man tilted his head, his gaze piercing even in the dim light. "A dangerous time to be traveling alone. Especially for a pretty young girl like yourself."

He began to creep towards her. Pho's blood ran cold.

Before he could say or do anything, another sound broke the tension – the distant clatter of hooves against the road. The man's expression shifted, and he glanced toward the source of the noise. He cursed.

Pho's instincts flared to life. She bolted for the trees, her pack jostling against her back. The man cursed under his breath but did not follow. She dove behind a thick cluster of ferns, her heart hammering as the hoofbeats grew louder. Through the gaps in the foliage, she saw the man standing resolutely in the middle of the road.

A group of riders emerged, their faces obscured by scarves and helmets. Bandits, she realized with a sinking feeling. The man exchanged a few terse words with them, his stance unwavering, although she could not make out the conversation. Pho could not tell if he was protecting her or just trying to keep her out of the bandits' sight for his own reasons.

Her mind raced. Should she stay hidden and hope the man meant her no harm? Or should she take her chances and run deeper into the jungle?

Run, said the voice in her head, although she swore it sounded different to the one she had been hearing.

That was enough for Pho, and she quietly started to make her way through the trees. After several minutes, knowing she was out of earshot of the man and the bandits, she decided to find a nook in the base of a tree to settle down for the night. She gulped as she looked into one small space she had found. The rainforests of Xudm were known to have a lot of exotic species of snake, the majority of which were poisonous, and Pho knew that running into one of those reptiles was the last thing she needed.

Her luck held, and she realised that nothing lived in these particular roots. She thanked the spirits, and tucked herself into the nook. She grabbed a small blanket from her pack and threw it over herself, hoping that it would shield her from the cold. Xudm was a tropical country, but it did get quite chilly in the evenings, and particularly in the early mornings before dawn. Sleep did not come easily for Pho, but eventually she drifted off into an uneasy doze, haunted by the echo of Luis' voice.

***

Crack!

Luis' hand came down onto Pho's cheek once more as she looked up at him from the floor.

"You have disrespected me and my authority for the last time!" he growled.

Pho was exhausted. Her body was scarred and violated, and she was unsure how much more she could take. Ever since Luis had found her on the road and brought her back to Phārā, it had been decided that she was to live with him permanently. Now he seemed to treat her like she was his object, doing whatever he wanted, whenever he wanted.

"Your father will be over for dinner tonight," said Luis curtly. "I expect you to be presentable for him, and I expect a home cooked meal for the both of us."

Pho looked at the floor and whispered, "Yes."

"What did you say, girl?" asked Luis in annoyance. "Louder! And use your manners!"

"Yes, sir," answered Pho.

The commander grabbed her chin and forced her to look into his eyes. "Good," he said. "You must learn to know your new place…"

Pho coughed, spluttered, and then opened her eyes. She was back in the jungle and she realised she was slumped in the nook of the tree she had sheltered under. Her cheek still burned from where Luis had hit her, and her skin still crawled. Wait. No, her skin was *actually* crawling. She screamed as she realised millipedes were walking all over her, and she jumped up in fear, trying her hardest to brush them all off. She nearly threw up as she noticed the amount of bugs that crawled in the space she had slept in last night. She dove over to her pack and hugged it tightly. What had she done? She was stupid. It had only just started to click that she was away from the road and lost in the huge expanse of rainforest that covered most of Xudm. How was she going to even get back to the road, let alone to Maṭṭā? She was lost, cold, and alone. If she stayed put, she would die. If she moved, she might still die – but at least she'd be fighting.

Chapter Fifteen

Josh looked flabbergasted at the three Herks before them. "Y-you?!" he stammered. "Captain Crysthan?!"

"We surrender," admitted Crysthan. "We come in peace!"

Drew looked at the Crownland Captain suspiciously. "What do you want?" he asked. "Why have you stowed away on our ship?" He shook his head. "How and when did you stowaway on our ship?"

"Well, the other day, we saw our chance and snuck aboard!" explained Irk.

"Yes Irk, that's enough," said Crysthan. "I'm sorry, Andrew Saran. I suppose we owe you an explanation."

"You could say that again," said Josh.

"You will discard all your weapons," commanded Drew. "And then join us in the cabin above deck for questioning."

Crysthan nodded. "As you wish," he said.

The looks of surprise on the faces of Geetie and Tenebrae were palpable as Drew and Josh led their prisoners into the cabin. Drew's eyes skirted to the left hand of Crysthan, which was missing four fingers from when then-Prince Lekt had tortured the Herk Captain following the Crownlands' assault on Wilder Forest. That was the instigating moment behind the tensions between Duchess Wilder and King Lekt. Drew remembered that Wilder had been livid at Lekt's use of torture against Crysthan, and the then-Prince's decision to force General Sylvia to arrest the Duchess was extremely inflammatory. Drew shook himself once more and focused on the situation at hand. Captain Crysthan of the Crownlands stood before them, Herk soldiers Irk and Murk beside him.

"General Sylvia did say that they were unable to find Murk," said Josh. "I guess it was to be expected that he would show up again."

Drew nodded. "Where did you slink off to?" he asked.

"Aw, well I hid for a bit in Cernsland actually," admitted Murk.

Crysthan rolled his eyes. "A Herk *never* reveals his secrets, you oaf!"

"Sorry, boss," said Murk.

"What are you doing here?" demanded Drew.

"We were looking for you," replied Crysthan. "I come with a warning."

"A warning?" asked Drew. "Why would a Herk of the Crownlands want to give me a warning?"

"About your uncle," continued Crysthan, unfazed by Drew's last comment.

"Count Michael?" asked Drew.

Thinking about his uncle made his blood boil. This was the man who had ordered the assasination of his father, who had caused his mother to exile herself in Wiln, and had therefore led to Drew being raised by Phil and Julia in the orphanage. He hated Count Michael with every inch of his body. It was almost more than his hatred of Grand Duke Shârvous. In fact, it probably was. This man had ruined his life.

"What about Count Michael?" asked Drew, again.

"He sees you as a threat, Saran," explained Crysthan. "Michael wishes to see the Crownlands expand into Harleland. He wishes to end the peace treaty and restart the war."

Anger coursed through Drew. Josh, Tenebrae and Geetie all looked shell shocked beside him. This *germ* had the audacity to try and cause yet another war between Harleland and the Crownlands? Not if Drew had anything to say about it. He envisioned himself leading a patrol of Protectors to the Black Fortress of the Crownlands and demanding the head of Count Michael. If Grand Duke Shârvous genuinely believed in the peace treaty he had signed last year with King Lekt, then he would give his traitorous Count up.

"Tell me all about Michael's plans," demanded Drew.

Crysthan shrugged. "He wishes to get his hands on these things called Weather Runes," he explained. Drew's mouth hung open, but he remained silent and allowed Crysthan to finish. "Right now, a ship of Herks assembled by Michael behind Shârvous' back is sailing to Xudm to collect the runes."

"And you came all this way and stowed away on our ship just to warn us?" asked Josh. "Why?"

"Because Count Michael is tearing our Sovereign Grand Dutchy apart from the inside," admitted Crysthan. "I respect you, Saran. I respect King Lekt. And I love Grand Duke Shârvous and my land. I want peace just as much as you do, and I believe we can be united against a common enemy."

Drew turned to his friends. "Can we trust them?" he whispered.

"We have no choice now," said Tenebrae. "What are we going to do, throw them overboard? They're here now, and whether we like it or not, they're coming to Xudm with us."

"Agreed," said Josh. "If they are being genuine, they will make useful allies against Count Michael."

"Drew!" said Geetie. "What if the person Octavia spoke about the other week was actually Count Michael and *not* Grand Duke Shârvous?"

Drew nodded. Perhaps Geetie was right. Was Count Michael after the runes, and not Shârvous? Or perhaps both were, and this was all a trick. His blood still boiled in anger when thinking about them, but he tried to calm himself.

"It's agreed then," said Drew. "We trust them – but keep an eye on them. They're still Herks at the end of the day."

The four friends agreed, and Drew turned back to the three Herks.

"We have decided to trust you," he announced. "But be warned, your every movement will be monitored."

Crysthan nodded. "So be it," he said. "And thank you. Together, we can ensure lasting peace for both the Crownlands and Harleland."

So it was that the three Herks were confined below deck. It was decided that Drew and Josh should be in charge of guarding them, the pair rotating every few hours or so to give the other a break. The shock of finding Crysthan and the others aboard had momentarily taken away their focus on the mission at hand – crossing the sea.

As it stood, they were now halfway there thanks to Geetie's seafaring skills. The jolly captain stood at the wheel humming sea shanties to himself while Drew and Tenebrae worked the ropes. Tenebrae had recovered from her sea sickness and had caught on well to how to rig the sail. Together, Drew and Tenebrae ensured the ship caught the maximum amount of wind to propel it towards Xudm as quickly as possible.

"Land ho!" called Geetie.

Excitement coursed through Drew. Here already?

"We've found ourselves an island!" called Geetie again.

That information did not surprise Drew considering they still had half the ocean left to sail, but the sight of land still lifted his spirits. It appeared to be a big island, with a large hill rising from the centre. Drew and Tenebrae climbed onto the bridge to join Geetie.

"This is the island that is placed in a different location on each map," explained Geetie. "I do not believe it has a name, but if I could have the honour, I think Mirage Island has a nice ring to it."

Tenebrae nodded. "I'd agree with that," she said. "We can add it to the archives in the Library of Lakton back in Boron Nigh."

"Strange though," said Geetie, looking at the four different maps he had. "I can deduce our exact location on these maps by looking at the sun relative to the clouds. I can tell you that all of these maps are wrong. This island is not in the same location as any of them."

"Mysterious," said Drew. "Perhaps it's a moving island?"

Tenebrae twitched. "Anyone else have the urge to investigate?"

Drew shook his head. "It seems interesting… But no, we have to get to Xudm as quickly as possible."

"Aw, come on Drew!" said Geetie. "It would take me under an hour to sail to the shore, and it would just be a little walk around. We may never get the opportunity to sail to this part of the world ever again!"

Drew sighed. "So be it," he said. "But make it quick! Octavia is relying on us."

"We haven't forgotten Octavia, but he's strong," said Tenebrae. "He will hold on for as long as it takes us to get back with the Ocean Sapphire." She sighed. "And I need to feel solid earth beneath my feet again before this sea sickness comes back."

So it was decided – they would investigate Mirage Island. Drew felt anxiety course through him. He prayed that Geetie and Tenebrae's side quest would not delay them too long. What if Octavia passed because they were held up exploring some random island? Drew realised that he would be unlikely to forgive either of them. As they sailed closer and closer to the island, the strong friendships between Drew, Tenebrae and Geetie came closer and closer to being tested.

Chapter Sixteen

Pho was exhausted. Mentally and physically exhausted. She had spent the last several hours slowly trudging through the rainforest, swearing every now and again that she recognised a certain tree or stream. That was because she was going in circles, and she knew it. She was hungry and her small supply of food she had crammed into her pack was already half eaten.

She had drank several times from the streams, and she was thankful that at least water was plentiful, despite the various other worries she had. She decided to rest for a bit by a small stream that passed under a fallen log. Small river stones and gravel created a nice little spot for her to sit for a while, safe from the bugs and critters that lived in the leaf litter of the forest floor, although she was weary of leeches. As she sat, the Sajak jewel fell from her robe and into the stream. She gasped as she saw it fall. But then, to her astonishment, the glowing blue stone began to react to the water. From the stream, the gemstone began casting blue beams of energy upward and out of the water, and before she knew it, a humanoid figure stood before her.

Pho stood up in terror and amazement. The figure motioned to her a symbol of peace, and then to her astonishment, it spoke.

"You are very, very brave, young Pho," it said, the vocals sounding like a distorted old man's voice. "It is imperative you bring the Ocean Sapphire to Mạttā, so it can be delivered to its rightful owner."

"A-are you the one who's been talking to me?" Pho asked, shaking in terror.

The figure shook its head. "I am afraid not," it replied. "I am Pogoda, the Demi-god of Weather."

"D-demi-god?" asked Pho. "A-and what do you mean by Ocean Sapphire? Is that its name?"

Pogoda nodded. "In your culture I am regarded as a spirit, and this object you refer to as one of the Sajak is indeed the Ocean Sapphire." He paused. "I never appear to a mortal unless the situation is dire, and now it is indeed at that point. I shall guide you back to the road, but it will be up to you from there to get to Maṭṭā."

Pho looked upon the spirit in awe. "Then if it wasn't you who's been speaking to me, who was? And who is the rightful owner of the Ocean Sapphire?"

A dark look came over Pogoda's face. "An evil not of this world…" he warned. He shook his head. "Do not have fear about that for now. More pressing is to give this sapphire to its rightful owner." He looked comfortingly at Pho. "You will know him when you see him."

With that, Pogoda dissipated, and the Ocean Sapphire stopped glowing. Pho rushed over to the stream and fished it from the bottom. The moment she held the stone in her hand, the voice of Pogoda spoke.

Turn to your left, Pho, it said. *Walk straight until I say otherwise. I will get you out of this, I promise…*

Pho felt hope course through her. She *would* survive after all.
Following the spirits' instructions, she turned to her left and
began to walk. After several minutes, she reached a rise. The
voice of Pogoda advised her to climb, and continue to the
right. After a good hour or so, Pho finally arrived back at the
road. Her relief was immeasurable, and she dropped to her
knees and cried.

"Thank you!" she cried, hoping Pogoda could hear.

There was silence. The spirit had left her for now it seemed,
but she felt buoyed by its presence thanks to the Ocean
Sapphire. She wondered who it was she would meet. Who
was the rightful owner of this stone? Perhaps he could tell
her more about the Sajak, and of Pogoda. Excitement raced
through her. Not only was she back on course to see her
sister in Mąttā, but she now knew she wielded a powerful
object that contained one of the spirits! She began to walk
along the road in the direction of her sister's village, hoping
that the journey would be as quick as possible. Pho did not
want to risk anymore delays.

After another hour of trekking along the road, Pho became
aware of the sound of hooves coming from back the way she
came. She jumped into the trees and hid herself from sight.
The last thing she needed would be a Belrench patrol
spotting her. If she got taken back to Phārā... To her relief, it
appeared that a family of fellow Xudists travelled together
on a single horse, an older couple and a young child. Pho got
an idea. Could she hitch a ride with these strangers? Even if
they were not headed to Mąttā specifically, she could at least
travel in that direction until they turned off onto another
road. Taking a deep breath, she stepped out. The horse

whinnied and came to a halt. A look of surprise came over the face of the old man as he spotted Pho.

"Hi!" said Pho cheerfully, despite her anxiety.

"Oh, what is a young girl such as yourself doing out here?"asked the man.

"I'm trying to get to Mạttā," explained Pho. "Um… would there be room on your horse?"

"Dear, this could be a trick by some bandits!" whispered the old woman, Pho overhearing the conversation.

"In broad daylight?" asked the old man. "These bandits are bold, but not that bold." He smiled at Pho. "I am Baddock, and this is my wife Lolo, and my son Ven. We are headed to Mạttā ourselves! Climb aboard, there's room."

"Thank you!" said Pho gratefully. "I appreciate it."

Pho climbed on the back of the horse behind Ven. The boy seemed the same age as Hax, and Pho felt a great deal of sadness wash over her knowing he had been forced to move. Perhaps with her newfound freedom, she could search for him and his mother.

"So, what brings you out here alone?" asked Baddock. "The wild is no place for young girls!"

"Well, I'm travelling to Mạttā to move in with my sister, Ara, actually," explained Pho. "I'm originally from Phārā!"

"Oh, Phārā," said Baddock. "We are from Ukik, on the east coast of Xudm." He sighed. "We're moving to Mạttā as well.

King Benjamin has transformed our once peaceful village into a resort for the Belrench."

"Don't give too much away!" pleaded Lolo. "We don't know if we can trust her yet!"

"She's a young girl, no more than sixteen!" retorted Baddock. "She is no danger to us."

"I'm Ven!" said the boy in front of her.

Pho smiled. She tried to forget about Lolo's suspicions and instead focused on conversing with Ven.

"I'm Pho," she replied. "Nice to meet you."

"Are you excited to move to Mạttā?" he asked. "I'm not. I loved living in Ukik. But King Ben has ruined everything for us there."

Pho's heart sunk. Her anger rose. King Ben had no right. His father King Mathieu had no right to colonise Xudm in the first place! One day, when she was old enough, Pho wished she could help do something about it. But the power of King Ben and the Belrench occupiers was so entrenched, she was unsure if it would ever be possible.

***

For the third or fourth time today, Pho thought again about what happened to the evil voice. Had Pogoda freed her of it somehow? She racked her brain and tried to think about who it belonged to. If Pogoda was a weather spirit, was this evil voice a dark spirit? Some sort of sinister spiritual force not of this world? She grew frustrated with her lack of knowledge, and Pogoda's lack of information. Here she was though, sitting comfortably behind Ven and bound for Mặttā, her earlier plight all but over.

The road ahead stretched in a dusty line between the towering trees, the midday sun filtering through their canopies in dappled rays. The rhythmic sound of the horse's hooves on the packed earth was soothing, almost hypnotic. Pho leaned back slightly, careful not to crowd Ven, and allowed herself to close her eyes for a moment. The Ocean Sapphire, now tucked safely into a hidden pocket, pulsed faintly against her chest, its warmth a subtle reminder of its presence.

Pho's mind churned with questions, as it always did. Who was the rightful owner of the Ocean Sapphire? What kind of person could command the respect of a spirit like Pogoda? And if there were other Sajak artefacts, where were they, and what powers did they hold? Most importantly, what role did she now play in the grander scheme of things?

Her thoughts were interrupted by Baddock's voice. "The road will split soon," he said. "One path to the east leads south, further inland; the other heads straight to Mặttā, by the coast. We should reach it by nightfall if we keep this pace."

Pho nodded absently, grateful for the family's hospitality but wary of the risks that came with her situation. She glanced at Lolo, who still eyed her with suspicion. While Pho understood the woman's caution, it stung to feel so distrusted, especially after the harrowing day she had had.

"Will you be staying with your sister long?" Ven asked, turning his head slightly to look at her.

Pho smiled. "I hope so. She's the only family I have left in Mạttā." Her voice faltered, and she quickly added, "It'll be good to see her again. It's been too long."

Ven nodded, his youthful curiosity not entirely satisfied but tempered by the gentle tone of her words. Pho looked up at the sky, now tinged with the golden hues of late afternoon. She felt a sense of unease creeping in, like the lingering shadow of the malevolent voice that had plagued her earlier. She glanced at the Ocean Sapphire hidden beneath her robes, wondering if it could sense her fears.

"Everything alright, Pho?" Baddock asked, his tone kind.

Pho forced a smile and nodded. "Just tired, that's all."

The family resumed their journey, and as they continued down the road, Pho couldn't shake the feeling that they were being watched. She glanced over her shoulder, scanning the treeline for any sign of movement, but there was nothing there – only the rustling leaves and the distant call of birds. They could not hear the group of six bandits closing in on them from behind.

Chapter Seventeen

Two small boats set out from *The Ocean Herald*, bound for Mirage Island. Drew watched from the back of his boat as Irk and Murk rowed, Captain Crysthan sitting at the front. In the other vessel, Josh and Tenebrae rowed, while Geetie watched ahead.

The ship was anchored far enough away from the shore that it could not be washed aground. Several minutes later, and the crew were making landfall on the island, parking their boats upon the beach. The hill in the centre of the island loomed large over them, while a rainforest hedged the top of the sand dunes.

"What are we going to do with these knuckleheads?" asked Josh, looking at the three Herks.

"Guard Irk and Murk on the beach," commanded Drew. "Captain Crysthan, you shall accompany Tenebrae, Geetie and I up into the jungle."

"As you wish," answered Crysthan curtly.

"Any funny business," said Josh, looking at Irk and Murk. "Any at all. And you'll wish you never snuck aboard our ship."

"You can trust us!" said Irk. "We ain't tryin' nothing!"

"Yeah!" agreed Murk.

Together, Drew, Tenebrae, Geetie and Crysthan ascended the sand dune and entered the rainforest. It was humid under the canopy of the trees. Drew felt sweat forming in every nook and cranny of his body, causing him to shake out his shirt uncomfortably.

"Drew, come take a look at this!" called Tenebrae.

Drew looked over to where his friend stood before what looked like a stone structure. Crumbling bricks seemed to be scattered around the ancient construction, but Drew gasped when he realised it was an entrance. A ruined staircase seemed to descend down into the dark.

"I wonder what's down there," whispered Tenebrae.

"Better not find out," said Drew, although he was certainly curious. "We don't want to awaken any ancient monsters or anything."

"What do these carvings mean?" asked Crysthan, looking at five strange shapes carved into the bricks.

Drew gasped. They were runes. He pulled out Octavia's parchment. Sure enough, the third line of runes on the parchment matched the five runes carved into this ancient doorway. They must be the Weather Runes.

"Could this be a shrine to the runes?" asked Drew.

"Look at the top!" said Geetie. "That looks like the carving of a stone."

"Perhaps it signifies the Ocean Sapphire?" wondered Tenebrae.

"Will we go in?" asked Geetie.

"Oh, I don't think I'm going in there," said Crysthan matter-of-factly.

"Oh, I think you are," said Tenebrae. "Big bad Herk Captain can't handle the dark?"

Crysthan bristled. Drew stopped himself from laughing, before commanding his prisoner to do as he was told.

"So be it," said Crysthan gruffly.

"I'll follow," said Drew. "Tenebrae, take the rear."

"Aye captain," replied Tenebrae sarcastically.

Down they went, down into the dark tunnel underneath the island.

***

It was cold. Very cold. There was very little light in the tunnel, only small shafts from the cracked ceiling giving the company any sense of vision. Drew was aware of several ancient carvings pertaining to the runes. At one point, the companions stumbled into a light-filled room, and Drew gasped as he saw a shrine with all twenty runes inscribed upon a great stone tablet.

As he approached, he noticed what appeared to be a drawing of a tower carved above the Shadow Runes. The Great Tower was referenced in this ancient place, as was the Green Tree above the Life Runes, and the same drawing of a stone from outside – likely the Ocean Sapphire – was carved above the Weather Runes.

But to his confusion, the last set of runes – the Death Runes, he remembered – had had their linked object or place carved over. Someone had vandalised the shrine, and this part of it in particular. Drew only knew two things about the Death Runes at this point. One, that they were from the lost Indigo Tower in the mythical southern land of Bespoke. And two, that they were lost to the world.

"All the runes are inscribed here," breathed Drew, turning to the others. But to his shock, the others stood silently, their hands in the air. To Drew's utter astonishment, several small glowing blue creatures wielding wooden spears appeared before Drew. He gasped as he realised that they floated in the air, and were devoid of legs. One of them shoved their weapon at Drew's chest.

"You are invading the sacred Temple of Nearth!" it called. "What business have you here?"

"Uh, we are…" stammered Drew. "We're travellers! We were just passing through."

"Not just anyone can pass through this place," said the blue thing. "Only one that carries the runes can even set foot upon this island."

Drew stared at the small, strange blue creature confused. "Well I… I do carry ten of them," he admitted.

The creature narrowed its eyes. "So he does carry them," it said.

It turned back to its companions and they whispered amongst themselves. Finally, it returned.

"I am Artsy, leader of the Sea Sprites," the creature said. "We are the ancient guardians of the Temple of Nearth."

"Can you move this spear away from me, please?" asked Tenebrae, exasperated.

Artsy looked at her in fury, but did not say anything. They commanded the other Sea Sprites to lower their weapons, and Drew's companions all had relief flood over their faces as they felt the spears move away from their necks.

"So, tell us what this is about?" commanded Crysthan. "How is this the Temple of Nearth? That was just a myth!"

"Silence!" commanded Artsy. "Only the rune bearer may speak in this sacred place."

"I ask the same question as him," said Drew. "The Temple of Nearth was supposedly lost below the sea millenia ago."

"Millenia ago, the Demi-god of Weather, Pogoda, realised that the power and greed of the ancient Kings of Nearth had grown too great," explained Artsy. "He offered them an ultimatum. Either give up the Ocean Sapphire and lose their powers – or their Temple and the lands around it would be flooded, and the High Race of Nearth would be wiped out forever."

"I suppose they chose the latter," suggested Drew.

"The last King of Nearth, Czmithicon, called Pogoda's bluff. He drowned, along with all his heirs, when the valley was flooded," Artsy said.

"Wow…" breathed Geetie. "The history is incredible!"

Artsy shot the food merchant a warning glance. Drew tried to ease the tension.

"We are on our way to Xudm," he explained. "We believe the Ocean Sapphire is in danger."

"The sapphire is lost!" cried Artsy in anger. "For an age, it was locked within a vault, deep within the Temple ruins. Guarded by the Žuvkozok, stone guards who never eat or rest, the perfect protectors of one of the four sets of runes." They sighed. "Pogoda spoke to us. He said the sapphire had washed ashore in Xudm."

"How did it become lost?" asked Drew. "If it were guarded by such powerful beings like these Žuv-what you call its, how did it get out? Or who got it out?"

Artsy's face looked sour. "He did," they said ominously.

"He?" echoed Drew. "That's what Octavia said, too. I thought he meant Grand Duke Shârvous at first, but now we think it might be Count Michael."

"These names mean nothing to me," answered Artsy. "Mere mortals perhaps, pretending they are bigger than they are." Now, the Sea Sprite flew close to Drew. "There are four sets of runes," they said, their voice dropping to a whisper. "You have two of them. If you are who I think you are, then you must find the other two. The fate of the world of Nearth is at stake!"

"We must get to Xudm," said Drew, urgency rising within him. "Pronto. Let's get back to Josh and those two dimwit Herks on the beach."

Artsy looked at Drew in horror. "You have more of you?" they said in shock. "But… surely you must have known! This island can only exist for others when they are in the presence of the rune bearer."

Geetie looked at Artsy in anger. "What's that supposed to mean then?" he asked. "My son is out there!"

"I'm sorry," replied the Sea Sprite. "But the moment the rune bearer left his sight, this island would have vanished for them. Gone in an instant into thin air." Artsy paused. "They'd have fallen into the sea."

With an urgency he had never felt before, Drew sprinted out of the ruined temple, Geetie, Tenebrae and Crysthan in his wake. They ran back through the rainforest and down the dunes onto the beach. To their horror, Josh, Irk and Murk were nowhere to be seen.

Chapter Eighteen

Pho screamed as a bandit grabbed her. Baddock shouted in anger as he fell off the horse, Lolo falling with him. Ven cried out in terror, the boy clinging onto the family horse as it bolted.

"Stop that mule!" shouted one of the bandits. "We can't let the guards in Maṭṭā become alerted!"

Baddock got to his feet and withdrew a knife. "Stay away from my family!" he yelled.

He punched one of the bandits. It was a good strike, and his foe collapsed. Pho jumped as she recognised one of the bandits as the strange man she had come across on the road the night before.

"Well, well, well," he said. "If it isn't the pretty little thing from last night. A shame you had to run from me."

Pho began backing away, trying to maneuver closer to Baddock.

"Leave her alone, you creep!" called Lolo.

Pho was thankful for her support despite Lolo's earlier mistrust.

"Oh, I don't think so," said the man. The other four standing bandits joined him in creeping closer to Baddock, Lolo and Pho. "I like this one," he said, staring at Pho.

He reached out and grabbed Pho's arm. She screamed and
kicked at him. Her foot made contact with his groin, and he
cried out in pain, momentarily losing his grip on her. That
was enough to allow Pho to wriggle her arm free of him and
bolt, Baddock and Lolo in her stead.

"Don't just stand there!" the man called. "After them!"

The other bandit who had been punched by Baddock had
come too, and he joined the other five in their pursuit. The
moon had risen by this point, and Pho sprinted terrified
along the dark road.

"We can't run forever!" cried Lolo. "Baddock, what are we
going to do?"

"You two go," he demanded. "I'll try and hold them off for
as long as possible."

"No!" screamed Lolo. "You can't! I can't lose you! What
about Ven?"

"You will give him a good life in Mąttā, I know it," replied
Baddock. "Go!"

Tears streaming down her face, Lolo reluctantly ran, Pho
beside her as Baddock stared down their pursuers.

"You want my family, you go through me!" called Baddock.

"Okay," replied one of the bandits nonchalantly.

Pho covered her ears as she heard the screams of Baddock.
Lolo screamed as the reality of what had just happened to
her husband hit home. Pho knew they had to keep running,

lest Baddock's sacrifice be in vein. They had put a fair
amount of ground between them and the bandits, but Pho
knew that they would catch up to them eventually – they had
horses, and the two terrified women did not.

"Let's hide in the trees," suggested Pho.

This would be the third time she would have to hide in the
jungle; it was becoming a regular thing at this point. But, just
as they snuck in behind some ferns, Pho saw a sight she
never expected to welcome. Belrench soldiers. Six or seven
of them, dressed in full armour, rode a steed each as they
called out to the bandits, who had now come back into view.
She and Lolo held each other close. Looks of terror came
over the bandits' faces and they scattered into the jungle,
each one being individually hunted by a Belrench soldier.
Pho and Lolo let go of each other and snuck out of the
jungle. Pho was not keen to be seen by the soldiers, but Lolo
hailed them down.

"Help, help!" she called.

One of the soldiers rode up to them. "Are you two okay?" he
asked. "Are you the ones who travelled with that boy? He
rode in on a horse alone, terrified."

"That's my son!" cried Lolo. "Those bandits jumped us.
They killed my husband…"

She sunk to the ground, her sadness echoing off the endless
expanse of trees on both sides of the road. The soldier looked
at her in sympathy.

"There, there," he said. "I'm sorry for your loss. But we should get you to the village and reunite you with your son."

"Yes," Lolo sobbed. "Please."

"And you, young lady?" he asked. "Are you this lady's daughter?"

"She's a stranger!" said Lolo suddenly. "We never had any trouble from bandits the entire way from Ukik until *she* came along!"

The soldier stared at Pho suspiciously. She gulped.

"We found her on the side of the road, wandering the jungle alone!" said Lolo, turning her anger onto Pho. "My husband was too kind for his own good, and it got him killed – we should have left you!"

"Okay, okay," said the soldier, separating Lolo from Pho. "We'll investigate this further back in Maṭṭā."

Pho stared at the ground. Perhaps Lolo was right. What if the bandits had tracked her, and it led them straight to this innocent family? Perhaps her earlier encounter with the man the previous night was a failed ploy, and the bandits had followed her looking for revenge. What if Baddock's death was her fault? Her mood was sombre as she climbed onto the back of one of the soldiers' horses. This entire plan had been a disaster. First, running away in the first place; second, thinking she could survive the dark road alone by herself; third, getting lost in the jungle as she tried to escape from the bandits; and now fourth, causing the death of a man who had just tried to help her, tearing apart a family who were just minding their own business. As she was transported closer to Mąttā, Pho wondered whether this was all worth it.

***

Mąttā was much bigger than Phārā. It felt more lively too, with the sounds of excited children running around filling Pho's ears. In Phārā, it would be quiet by this time of night, but here there seemed to be a festival taking place. The main street was lined with traditional Xudist lanterns, and dancers wearing bright silks performed in a parade.

"You've come to Mąttā in the middle of the annual Water Festival," explained the soldier. "The locals here celebrate the water, and of course their weather spirit."

Pho looked down at her robes, where the Ocean Sapphire sat safely. What would these festival-goers think if they knew she held the Sajak that corresponded with the spirit? Eventually, the soldier took the two exhausted women into a small building. This was supposedly an office for the Belrench soldiers. A very formal looking Belrench man sat at a desk and beconned the pair over to him.

"I will leave you for now," said the soldier. He turned to Lolo. "My colleague will assist you in being reunited with your son."

Lolo nodded at the soldier as he left the office.

"Names?" asked the man behind the desk.

"Um, Pho."

"Lolo."

"Ah, Lolo," said the man. "We have your son, Ven, here."

From another room, Ven raced out to embrace his mother.

"Oh, my boy!" cried Lolo.

"Where's father?" asked the boy.

Lolo looked stricken. "He saved us from the bandits," she explained. "But to do that, he had to stay behind."

"Oh…" replied Ven. "Well, when's he coming back?"

Lolo teared up. Pho did too. She could not contain herself. Tears flowed down her face. Her heart was being shattered as she witnessed this grief-stricken mother tell her child that his father would never come home. She turned to the man at the desk. She could not witness anymore.

"So, Pho you said?" he asked. "Hmm, we have no record of a Pho in Mattā. Do you have family here?"

"My sister," Pho replied. "Her name is Ara."

The man poured through his records. "Ah yes, we have an Ara. I shall call her down here to collect you, child."

Pho's heart sang. Finally, she was going to see her sister again. After so, so long, Pho would be free.

Chapter Nineteen

Geetie dropped to his knees. He screamed. Drew stood and looked around in frustration. Surely, somewhere, his friend would be waiting for them. Perhaps Josh just took Irk and Murk to find some water. Another thought occurred to him. What if they went back to the ship? But to Drew's dismay, both boats the party had used to paddle to the island still sat grounded upon the beach.

Drew looked over at Tenebrae. She seemed stricken. Captain Crysthan hung his head, seeming to mourn the loss of his Herk comrades.

"I am sorry," said the voice of Artsy. The Sea Sprite must have followed them back to the beach. They floated above the ground, giving each companion a sympathetic look.

"Tell me!" roared Geetie, as he confronted Artsy. The food merchant had got to his feet and now he stood directly in front of the Sea Sprite, his face centimeters away. "What happened to my son?"

Artsy did not flinch. "I'm sorry, my friend," they replied. "Your son, and your two prisoners, would have been deposited into the sea."

Geetie went to swing at Artsy, but the Sea Sprite flew clear.

"I am not to blame for the workings of this island," Artsy said. "However, I give you this hope – the Sea of Many Currents, as you call it, is known as such because of its many powerful currents." They paused. "The Ley Line, which gives both us Sea Sprites as well as the Weather Runes powers, runs directly below this island."

"But the island moves," said Drew. "Does that mean the Ley Line moves too?"

"How does this *bullshit* help?!" screeched Geetie, his face red with anger and tears.

"The island moves to different points along the Ley Line," said Artsy, quickening his speech. "The current around the island is influenced by the direction of the Ley Line. If your son is lucky, he'll be swept off by the current straight toward the coast of Xudm."

"But we're still a good day or more from Xudm!" cried Geetie. "He won't survive that long! He might have already drowned! What if a shark gets him?"

"Geetie, there's nothing we can do–" began Tenebrae as she went to comfort him; but, she was cut off by the devastated food merchant.

"What do you mean, nothing we can do?!" he screeched. "Fat lot of good you've done anyway Tenebrae! Complain, complain, complain, and then she spends all day in bed *sea sick!*" His voice dropped to a whisper as all present stared at Geetie in shock. "It should have been *you* on the beach…"

Drew's mouth opened in shock. Tenebrae stood quietly as she looked back at Geetie. "Maybe it should have been…" she replied meekly.

Geetie started panting, clearly having a panic attack. He once more dropped to his knees. "No, no, no," he cried. "I didn't mean to... I'm a stupid, fat oaf!"

Drew ran over to his friend and embraced him. "You're not stupid," said Drew, looking at the distraught man.

Geetie wiped away his tears. "I couldn't protect my son," he sobbed.

"It wasn't your fault," replied Drew. "None of us knew."

"We should never have come here!" screamed Geetie. Then he looked at Drew guiltily. "Sorry..." he whispered.

Drew shook his head. "It was my fault," he said. "My apprentice is lost because I wasn't a good mentor. I should have been with him on the beach. I left him to fend for himself..."

Tears flowed freely down their faces. Drew and Geetie slumped on the beach in utter defeat. Tenebrae looked ghostlike, not a breath of life in her face, as if her entire world was about to end. Crysthan watched them in sympathy, understanding apparent within him that the young man he had barely known had meant so much to his three new companions.

"I think... I just need some space," said Geetie after several silent moments.

Drew nodded. He rose from the sand and approached Tenebrae.

"Are you okay?" Drew asked. She was still shaken.

"No," she replied. "Geetie was right. We shouldn't have come here... If I wasn't sea sick–"

Crysthan cut her off. "You need to stop blaming yourselves," he said as he came to stand next to them. "I understand you're all devastated with what's just happened to Josh."

"We are," replied Drew, tears still in his eyes. A great wave of sadness and pain began to tear through him. His friend was actually dead. There seemed no way he could have survived.

"There's still hope, Saran," said Crysthan. "I refuse to give up on Irk and Murk. And if I can help you to find your friend Josh as well, I will."

"Thank you," replied Drew. "That means a lot."

"I am sorry for what has happened here," said Artsy. "Drew, I need you to listen to me carefully. Regardless of what has happened to Josh, those Weather Runes need to be collected. They are in great danger."

The Sea Sprite repeated the prophecy given to them by Kora:

Across a blue ocean, with many flows,

To Xudm's lands, an evil grows,

A child keeps the Ocean Sapphire,

But to end the dark, one must know,

Defeat the evil, and another will grow.

"The Ocean Sapphire is in the hands of a child…" said Drew.

Artsy nodded. "She is in great peril. If she is found by King Benjamin's men, the sapphire could fall into the greedy hands of the Belrench. And then nothing will stop…" They shuddered. "*Him* from getting it."

"We will go at once," said Drew. "Thank you, Artsy."

Tenebrae and Crysthan boarded one boat, while Drew and Geetie boarded the other. Drew thought it best to keep Geetie and Tenebrae apart for the time being following what had just happened on the beach. Drew sighed as he looked back at the shore. He raised his hand in farewell to Artsy and then turned back to the sea. They began to row toward *The Ocean Herald*.

***

"I don't think we should give him false hope," said Drew, as he, Tenebrae and Crysthan sat around the small table below deck.

The Herk Captain nodded. "In my experience, if he starts hoping, then it will make his grief even more pronounced when it turns out his son really is gone." He sighed. "Despite my own hope for Irk and Murk, I won't let myself get too excited."

Drew drank from his mug. They had all poured themselves mead from the barrels below deck, hoping the alcohol would help numb the pain of losing Josh. Geetie rested upstairs in the cabin, entirely unable to bring himself to captain the ship. Drew had locked the wheel in place to ensure *The Ocean Herald* would continue to shoot directly for Xudm. They were due to arrive by noon the next day. In fact, they would almost be in Belrench waters by this point. Drew shuddered as he imagined being intercepted by a Belrench Navy vessel.

"Even if we get past the Navy," said Tenebrae. "Where do we even start looking for the runes? It's not a massive country, but it won't be any small feat."

"The sapphire is in the hands of a child," said Drew. "I have no doubt that being in possession of runes for long enough will make a child go crazy."

"We need to try and befriend the locals," suggested Crysthan. "Then we can try and deduce which child may hold the runes."

"There's a lot of villages in Xudm," Tenebrae pointed out. "It will take a long time to search them all."

Drew sighed. He had a sinking feeling that they would not find the Ocean Sapphire in time to save Octavia. He could not lose two friends. He *would* not. With determination, Drew stood before Tenebrae and Crysthan.

"We *are* going to find the child," he announced. "I know deep down we will. Octavia is relying on us."

Crysthan looked up at Drew with respect. Tenebrae nodded.

"We've lost Josh – but we won't lose anyone else," continued Drew. "Tomorrow, we land in Xudm. And tomorrow, we find the Ocean Sapphire."

Chapter Twenty

Pho had never felt so happy in her life as she saw her sister walk toward her.

"Pho!" cried Ara, as she embraced her sibling. A surreal feeling coursed through Pho. She was actually here. "What are you doing here!? How did you get here alone? I was flabbergasted before when the soldier came around and told me you were here alone!"

"I…" sobbed Pho. "I had to leave."

The emotions that flooded through her overwhelmed Pho. All the trials, all the challenges, and here she was. Free at last, and her sister before her. Pho almost laughed, and then she began to sob.

"It's okay," soothed Ara, beaming at seeing Pho again. "Come on, let's get back to my place. I'll put some tea on, and you can tell me everything."

Pho nodded gratefully. She followed her sister through the festival and onto a quiet back street. Yet another wave of relief and happiness flowed through her. She felt joy in being in Ara's company and finally away from the road and jungle that had challenged her.

A row of houses lined the street, and it was into one of these that Ara led Pho. Inside it was nice and cosy, a fire burning in the fireplace to the side. A man – Ara's husband – sat in a chair by the fire. He stood and walked over to the pair in greeting.

"Pho!" he said. "Well this is a surprise!"

"Hello, Rith," replied Pho. "It's been a while."

Rith smiled. "Hasn't it what!" he agreed. "Look, I have some light food prepared if you're hungry."

"Yes, please," said Pho, realising she had not eaten since she used the last of her supplies back in the rainforest when she was lost.

Ara put the kettle on to boil, and then sat down with Pho by the table.

"I ran away," admitted Pho, looking down.

She was unsure if her sister would harshly judge her or not for her decision, and she prepared herself for the worst. But when she looked up again, she noticed Ara stared at her in sympathy.

"I almost ran away, years ago," Ara admitted.

"Oh," replied Pho, surprised.

"Our father wanted me to marry a Xudist warlord who had passed through the area," she admitted. "He told me the decision was out of my hands."

"He never mentioned that…" said Pho.

"Instead I married one of the men who helped to defeat the warlord." Ara smiled and looked over at Rith.

"I heard something about Rith fighting a warlord," said Pho. "But our father trying to marry you off to him?"

"I told him where to stick it, that's for sure," said Ara. "He seems to think I didn't love him. He thinks that's why I defied his choice of husband and then left for Mạttā."

"He does not believe in freedom of choice," said Pho. "He's so hung up on status that he forgets what's actually important – the happiness of his family."

"Why did you run away?" asked Ara. "He tried to marry you off, too?"

"Yes," admitted Pho. "Commander Luis is a high-ranking member of the Belrench army who is stationed in Phārā. He's in line to become our next Lord. Our father wanted the same status afforded to us that the Belrench get."

Ara shook her head. "Here in Mạttā, I have seen many young women married off to Belrench officers and commanders. Each time, the girl's family is forgotten about. They never get the status promised to them." She sighed. "And the poor young woman is treated as an object for the rest of her sad life."

A deep hatred for Belrance coursed through Pho. The disgusting behaviour of this sad Kingdom and their ongoing occupation of this peace-loving land made her blood boil.

"Do you think I made the right decision?" asked Pho. "To run away?"

"It was an explosive option," said Ara. "And our parents will find it hard to forgive you – at least our father will." She sighed. "Ultimately in the long term, this is the right decision." Then she smiled. "You have a place here to call home."

Pho's heart filled with warmth. "Thank you," she sobbed, embracing her sister. "That's all I've ever wanted."

The sisters talked and laughed for the rest of the night. Pho felt happiness surge through her, and she felt relaxed and comfortable for the first time in months.

***

It was a beautiful day as Pho wandered down to the beach. It had been so long since she was able to freely walk down to the shore, and Pho relished her newfound freedoms. Children played in the waves while parents sat together talking higher on the beach. Pho walked down below the waterline, allowing the waves to gently lap at her feet. It was a long beach, a large headland up the opposite end. It seemed at least four kilometers to walk, and Pho was up for the challenge. Ara had encouraged her to rest after her long and difficult journey to get here, and despite sleeping in, Pho had decided she needed to feel the ocean breeze in her hair again.

On she walked, clearing about one and a half kilometers within the first half an hour. No one else had come this far up the beach, and Pho was enjoying the quiet serenity, broken only by the crashing waves beside her. She squealed in glee when she spotted a huge clam shell, and she quickly scooped it up. This would be the first in her new collection. Her heart ached at losing her original collection, back at her parents house. Perhaps one day, when she was older and more capable of defending herself, she would travel back to Phārā and gather them. She put the clam into her inner robe pocket, where the Ocean Sapphire still sat.

She had not heard from either the evil voice nor from Pogoda in days, and she wondered if they would ever show themselves again. Just at that moment, Pho spotted something in the water. She squinted her eyes. Was it a fish? No, it seemed too big. A shark? She had often observed sharks from the beach back in Phārā, and they just seemed like fascinating creatures. Maybe not if you encountered one in the water, but observing them from a safe distance was a lot of fun, in Pho's opinion. But then the thing in the water seemed to get thrown closer, until it was washed up on the beach. Then Pho's blood ran cold. This was a person. A young man, around her age, wrapped in a soaked black garment. She ran over to him and checked to ensure he was okay. She gasped. He was not breathing and his face was pale. This man was dead. Pho stood, took a step back and covered her mouth.

Just at that moment, she heard a shout. Two other men were hurtling towards her. They wore strange armour she did not recognise. Pho was not interested in finding out more, and she decided to dash in the other direction.

"It's Josh!" called one of them. They both knelt down by the young man. "He's... he's dead," said one of them.

"What are we gonna do without him? We can't find the runes if he's dead!" called the other.

"No, wait! He still has a pulse!"

Pho stopped running and turned back. Perhaps she should help these people. She was unsure who they were and where they came from, but she did not want to leave this man they called Josh to die if there was still hope.

"Um," she said, approaching them. "C-can I help at all?"

"Appreciate the sentiment, love," said one. "But I don't see how a young girl like yourself can help."

Just at that moment, a strange feeling came over Pho. Like an instinct. She involuntarily reached into her robe and produced the Ocean Sapphire. The two men stared at the stone in wonder, as Pho placed it onto Josh's chest. The sapphire exploded into colour, blue mixed with purple, green, yellow, red and all other manner of bright colours. And then he spluttered and sat up. Pho collected the jewel from him and placed it back in her robes.

"Wh-what…" breathed Josh. He looked around, flabbergasted. "Irk? Murk?" He stared at Pho. "Wh-who are you?" He laughed. "I'd say I'm in heaven but you two *bozos* are here."

"Oi!" called Irk. "Who are you calling a bozo?"

"I think I should be asking who *you* are," said Pho, breaking up their little reunion.

"I am Josh," said the young man. "Josh Gunnersbury, a Protector of Harleland." He looked over at Irk and Murk. "These two are Herks of the Crownlands."

"Oh," said Pho. "Harleland? You've come a long way… My name is Pho. And wait. Wasn't there some sort of war between you two? Why are you here together?"

"It's a long story," said Murk.

"Pho, how did you do that before?" asked Irk. "With that blue stone thing, and making it go all flashy and stuff."

"Blue stone thing?" asked Josh. "What blue stone thing?"

Pho suddenly felt defensive. This Josh guy better not be after the Ocean Sapphire. Suddenly a memory came back to her. She would meet the rightful owner of the Ocean Sapphire soon, according to Pogoda. Was Josh Gunnersbury that rightful owner?

"Let's get you back to the village," said Pho. "We can talk more there."

Josh and the two Herks agreed, and the four new companions set off back for Mạttā. Pho felt excitement course through her. Her questions about the Ocean Sapphire were about to be answered – she could feel it.

Chapter Twenty-One

By the time the Belrench Navy had spotted *The Ocean Herald*, Drew, Tenebrae, Geetie and Crysthan had already made landfall in Xudm. The four companions stood now on the beach, their dinghy parked upon the shore again like on Mirage Island, as they awaited the incoming marines. Geetie stood quietly, while Drew and Crysthan put their heads together.

"As we agreed before," said Drew. "We are a joint diplomatic mission of Harleland and the Crownlands for trade in Xudm."

"Agreed," said Crysthan, the Herk Captain looking at Drew seriously as the leader of the patrol arrived.

"Welcome to Belrance," he said. "I note by the style of your vessel that you are from Harleland. What brings you to our Kingdom?"

"Trade," said Crysthan. "We are jointly sent by King Lekt of Harleland and Grand Duke Shârvous of the Crownlands to set up a trade post here on the coast of Xudm."

"The Harlelish and the Crownlands working together," said the leader. "Well I never. Your war truly is over then?"

"We live in peace now," said Drew, choosing not to explain the underlying tensions between the two lands. "Will you take us to the nearest village? And then organise a meeting with King Benjamin's vassal here in Xudm?"

"Well, you appear to be in luck," said the leader. "For we have recently celebrated the appointment of a new vassal here in Xudm. He does so happen to live in the nearest village. Come. Let us take you to Phārā."

They set out, walking up the shore towards the village. Drew could just make out houses on the upper part of the beach, however still a fair way down.

"How was the trip?" asked the leader. "The Sea of Many Currents has a formidable reputation."

"If it were not for Geetie here, we would have lost our way," said Drew.

Geetie said nothing, the heart broken man continuing to walk in silence. Tenebrae looked at Drew in concern.

"He still hasn't said a word since Josh vanished," she said.

Drew shook his head. "Josh was his entire world," he replied. "I don't think Geetie can ever be the same again."

Tenebrae hung her head sadly. She was clearly still upset at Geetie's words yesterday, and Drew knew it had opened up emotional scars inside her.

"How are you, Tenebrae?" he asked. "After what happened yesterday?"

She shook her head. "I don't know," she admitted. "I think I just need to think it all over."

She slowed her pace as if to drop to the back of the group, giving Drew the hint that she was not ready to talk just yet.

A hollow feeling opened up within him. Octavia was dying, Josh was gone, and now Geetie and Tenebrae had a rift between them. Was this the end of the friend group that Drew had thought would last forever?

***

"Ah, Phārā!" said the leader as the group entered the village. "Allow me to find our new Lord – I am unsure if he will have time to hear your proposition, what with getting the lay of the land when it comes to ruling and all, but I will try nonetheless."

"Thank you," said Drew gratefully.

He looked around the village square. The entire place was brimming with culture. Lanterns hung off the roofs of the buildings, market stalls lined the alleyways, and people seemed to crisscross the square, going this way and that. There was just one thing that seemed odd, and that was the amount of Belrench soldiers that seemed to be stationed in the village. Drew noticed the suspicious stares the locals seemed to throw at the soldiers as they walked past.

"I don't like this," said Tenebrae. "This feels like an occupation."

Drew nodded. "The way that these people look at those soldiers…"

"It reminds me of the Crownlands," said Crysthan. Drew turned to him in shock. "It reminds me of the way we used to look at the Harlelish Protectors," finished the Herk Captain.

Drew opened his mouth to speak, but nothing came out. Was Crysthan right? Was *Harleland* the oppressors of the Crownlands, before the war?

"Make way!" came a call. "All hail the Lord of Xudm, his honourable representative and vassal of King Benjamin the Great!"

A tall and handsome man, around his mid-thirties Drew could deduce, stood before them. As Drew went to speak, a local man approached them. He looked at King Ben's vassal.

"Commander Luis!" he said. "How has the search for my daughter gone?"

"It's Lord now, actually," replied Luis. "I have accepted King Ben's recent invitation to become Lord of Xudm – Chip, you know better than to interrupt someone of status such as myself. You shall wait for me to finish with these strangers."

The man called Chip looked at Luis in shock.

"L-lord?!" he spluttered in shock, but he was grabbed on the back by a soldier, causing Chip to bow and move away to wait. Lord Luis approached Drew.

"So, I am told that King Lekt of Harleland wishes to treat with me and my Kingdom," he said.

The way he looked at Drew, as if he was a lesser being, made his skin crawl.

"King Lekt of Harleland and Grand Duke Shârvous of the Crownlands have sent a joint diplomatic mission to negotiate a trade deal," lied Drew. "Captain Crysthan represents the Crownlands."

Crysthan nodded. "I hope our talks can be constructive, my Lord," he said.

"Hmm," replied Luis. "Interesting indeed. I could potentially negotiate an agreement. But come! The middle of a village is no place for trade negotiations, and we don't want to be interrupted by the common folk."

He shot a glance at Chip. Tenebrae scowled, and even Crysthan had a look of disgust on his face. Geetie said nothing, but Drew could see a look of dislike in the food merchant's eyes.

"Okay, move on," commanded a soldier, herding the four companions after Lord Luis.

"Please, sir!" said Chip, running up to Drew and grabbing his arm. "My daughter is missing! She's been gone almost a week, and Commander Luis – *Lord* Luis – as her fiance promised me he would find her!"

Drew looked at the man in sadness. "I'm sorry about your daughter," he replied. "But–"

He was cut off by a soldier grabbing Chip and dragging him away.

"Do not interfere with Lord Luis' trade discussions!" yelled the soldier.

Drew looked at Tenebrae. "These Belrench people seem to think they have control over the locals," he said.

"It's horrible," replied Tenebrae. "What did that Chip guy ask you about?"

"Apparently his daughter went missing a week ago," explained Drew. "And this Luis guy was meant to find her, but hasn't."

"I expect his public service to be near zero," said Geetie suddenly. He looked at Drew and Tenebrae as they continued to walk. "I lost my son, and I don't want another parent to lose their child. I think we should help him."

"We–" began Drew, before being cut off by Tenebrae.

"Come on, Geetie, we'll go together," she suggested. "Drew and Crysthan can handle the negotiations."

Drew nodded. "Very well," he said.

But as Geetie and Tenebrae went to leave, they were stopped by a soldier.

"You will all be present for Lord Luis to question," he said gruffly.

A look of anger came over Geetie. "You have no control over me!" he spat.

The soldier unsheathed his sword and held it at Geetie's throat.

"Choose your next words wisely," he suggested. "No one speaks to a soldier of Belrance in such a derogatory manner."

Suddenly, Drew's blood ran cold. He exchanged a look with Crysthan, who nodded in understanding. They were surrounded on all sides by soldiers, and were herded like sheep toward Lord Luis' manor, which sat on the outskirts of the village.

"This feels like more an arrest than a peaceful trade negotiation," whispered Crysthan.

Drew nodded in agreement. A sombre feeling fell over the companions as they crossed a well-tended lawn to the entrance of the manor. As they entered the mansion, a feeling of dread came over him. What would happen if they truly were detained, and unable to search Xudm for the Ocean Sapphire?

Chapter Twenty-Two

Pho carefully poured tea for the three weary travelers, her movements steady despite the lingering tension in the room. Sitting across from them, she tried to gauge their intentions. Her sister Ara had been wary about letting the strangers into their home – a caution Pho shared but eventually set aside. Ara's reluctance lingered like a shadow, but Pho's curiosity outweighed her caution. She studied Josh as he sipped his tea. Despite his youth, his eyes hinted at a life filled with trials and triumphs.

"So, what happened?" she asked. "What brought you to Xudm, and how did you end up overboard?"

Murk shifted in his seat, setting his teacup down. "Well, it wasn't exactly overboard," he began, glancing at his companion. "The island we were on... it just vanished. Beneath our feet."

"Poof! Gone into thin air!" Irk interjected, throwing his hands up dramatically.

"We found ourselves swimming in the middle of the ocean," Murk concluded with a wry smile.

Josh sighed, his expression heavy with concern. "I'm worried about my father, and Drew, and the others. What if they were swept in a different direction?"

"Poor Captain Crysthan," Irk muttered. "With any luck, they'll wash ashore too."

Pho's brows knit together. "There are others?" she asked.

Josh nodded. "Yes, four of us set out from Harleland: my father Geetie, my mentor Drew, Tenebrae, and myself." He gestured to the Herks. "These two, along with their Captain, Crysthan, were stowaways."

Irk cleared his throat. "We were following orders."

Josh rolled his eyes. "Hard to believe Shârvous sent Herks to help us find the runes."

"Runes?" Pho echoed, struggling to follow the flood of unfamiliar names and terms.

Josh leaned forward. "Yes, ancient artifacts. That's why we're here – to search Xudm for some of them." He smiled warmly. "Thank you for the tea, Pho, but we should be on our way."

Pho hesitated. Her thoughts churned. Pogoda's prophecy, the Ocean Sapphire's strange return to her possession, and now these travelers' arrival – it could not all be coincidence, could it?

"Wait," she said, her voice trembling slightly. "This artifact you're looking for… is it called the Ocean Sapphire?"

Josh's eyes widened. "You know of it?"

Pho fumbled with her robes, drawing out the sapphire. Its ethereal blue light pulsed, illuminating the room in a soft glow. Josh stared, his expression a mixture of awe and disbelief.

"Well," he said after a pause. "That's convenient."

Before anyone could react, Irk lunged at Pho, tackling her to the ground. She screamed as the sapphire slipped from her grasp, landing on the floor. Murk scooped it up swiftly.

"Our gracious Lord will be much obliged, Josh," Irk sneered, unsheathing his blade. He positioned himself between Josh and the exit, his stance ready for a fight.

Josh's face contorted with rage. "You've been deceiving us this whole time?"

Murk's laughter was sharp and grating. "As if the Grand Duke would ever send Herks to aid you!" he mocked. "Nothin' personal Josh, we're just following orders."

Josh went to lunge after Murk, but Irk stopped him. The Herk kicked at Josh, sending him flying backward into the table.

"We did tell the truth about one thing," said Irk. "There *was* a ship of Herks sailing to Xudm to get the runes! And now, here we are, courtesy of *The Ocean Herald*. Come on, Irk. Let's go."

Josh watched helplessly from the floor as the Herks fled, the sapphire now in their possession.

"They stole it!" Pho exclaimed, her voice shaking. "I have to get it back! You don't understand what powers it holds!"

Josh groggily got up and rubbed the back of his head.

"I know exactly what powers it holds!" Josh snapped, slamming his fist on the table. "That sapphire contains the five Weather Runes. If Shârvous gets his hands on it…" He trailed off, running a hand through his hair in frustration.

Ara appeared at the top of the stairs, drawn by the commotion. "What's going on?"

Josh turned to Pho. "How did you come by the sapphire?"

Pho took a deep breath. "My friend, Hax, found it in a cave near Phārā. He gave it to me as a gift. But strange things happened. I heard voices – one evil and another claiming to be Pogoda, the weather spirit."

Josh's eyes widened. "Pogoda spoke to you?" He looked stricken. "And an evil voice… perhaps the same one that haunted Drew…"

Pho looked at Josh in disbelief. "This Drew – does he also hold runes?"

"Yes," Josh replied grimly. "I hope you meet him someday. But right now, I need to find a weapon and recover that sapphire. Thank you, Pho. You were brave to keep it safe for so long. Now it's up to me."

He left the house and set off. Pho set off after him.

***

"What are you doing here?" asked Josh, looking at Pho in confusion.

He stood at the outskirts of Mạttā, and Pho had managed to catch up to him before he stepped outside of the village. She had overheard him asking some of the villagers what direction the Herks took off in, and it seemed they were headed for Phārā.

"I have to get the sapphire back," she answered. "I'm part of this now, whether either of us like it or not."

Josh smiled at her. "Oh very well," he said. "Just don't get yourself into trouble."

"I mean I can try," replied Pho. "No guarantees though."

Josh smirked at her. "Hmm, you definitely seem like trouble," he said. "Okay, follow me! And keep up!"

"Do you know where you're going?" asked Pho. "After all, you're not exactly local."

"You make a good point," replied Josh.

"Maybe you *do* need me then," Pho pointed out.

"We'll see," said Josh with a wry smile. "Well, tour guide, tell me where this road goes."

Pho stared down the road with a sinking feeling in her chest.

"It leads to my home village of Phārā," she explained.

Josh could clearly see the sad look on her face. He smiled at her.

"I take it that you had a bad experience there," he said softly.

Pho nodded. "I ran away from my parents and my fiancé," she explained. "I have to be free, Josh. I couldn't be forcibly married off like my father wanted. So I came here to live with my sister."

Josh nodded. "I understand," he said. "I'm sorry that happened, and I hope you can find peace here in Mạttā." He sighed. "Last year, my father and I had our house burnt to the ground by the Herks of the Crownlands." Pho noticed a tear form in his eye. "It's rebuilt now, thanks to the peace treaty between our two lands. But..." he trailed off. "But what happens if Irk and Murk get that sapphire back to the Crownlands? Will Shârvous use them to try and invade Harleland?" A look of fear and emotional pain came over his face. "What happens if our home is destroyed again?"

Pho patted him on the back. "We'll fix it," she said. "We'll get that sapphire back! Come on, let's go."

Josh looked over at a nearby stable. There seemed to be a commotion going on, and Pho had a feeling one of the steeds had been stolen.

"How much for a horse?" asked Josh, approaching the stableboy.

"Six hundred baht to rent," he demanded.

"I'm going after those thieves," explained Josh. "They stole a very valuable object of ours, and if I can get your horse back from them as well, I will."

"Get our horse back, and it's free," said the stableboy, looking at Josh and Pho in hope.

Josh nodded. "Very well," he said.

With that, Josh and Pho climbed upon a grey horse and took off from Mąttā, Pho's breath catching in her throat as she realised she would inevitably come face to face with her father and Commander Luis once again.

Chapter Twenty-Three

Drew could feel the unease hanging in the air as they were led into Lord Luis' manor. The interior was lavishly decorated with tapestries bearing the emblem of King Benjamin the Great – a golden lion against an indigo background. The opulence contrasted sharply with the stark expressions of the soldiers and the simmering resentment among the locals.

Lord Luis gestured toward an ornate table in the center of the room. "Please, take a seat," he said, his tone both commanding and dismissive.

Drew hesitated but complied, as did Crysthan. Geetie and Tenebrae remained standing, their postures tense. The soldier who had threatened Geetie lingered by the door, his hand resting on the hilt of his sword.

"First to the introductions. I am Lord Luis Occitanie, Ruler of Xudm and vassal of King Ben." He looked disinterestedly at Drew and the others. "Now, let us discuss this trade agreement." He leant back in his chair. "You claim to represent both Harleland and the Crownlands. An unusual alliance, considering your recent history."

"Unusual, perhaps," said Crysthan, maintaining a diplomatic tone. "But not impossible. Both our nations see the value in establishing peaceful trade routes and mutually beneficial agreements."

Lord Luis smirked. "Peaceful trade routes. How noble. And yet, one must wonder what truly motivates such a partnership." His gaze lingered on Drew. "Tell me, what goods do you seek to trade? And what do you offer in return?"

Drew opened his mouth to respond but was interrupted by the sound of shouting outside. The soldier by the door stepped out to investigate, leaving the group momentarily alone with Lord Luis.

"We offer fine textiles, spices, and crafted goods," Drew said quickly, seizing the moment. "In return, we hope to acquire rare materials from Xudm – pearls, exotic woods, and perhaps even your renowned wine."

Lord Luis' eyes narrowed. "A reasonable proposal. But such trade requires trust. And trust, my friends, is in short supply."

Before Drew could respond, the door burst open. The soldier returned, dragging a disheveled man into the room. The man's face was bruised, and his clothes were torn. "My Lord," the soldier said. "This man was caught attempting to incite unrest in the village square."

Lord Luis' expression darkened. "Unrest? Explain yourself."

The man struggled against the soldier's grip. "I was only speaking the truth! Your soldiers take more than they give. They patrol our streets like we're prisoners in our own homes. And my daughter is still missing, yet you do nothing!"

Drew's stomach turned as he recognised the man. It was Chip, the desperate father they had encountered earlier. Geetie stepped forward, his fists clenched. "Let him go," he demanded. "He's grieving and looking for justice. That is not a crime."

The soldier tightened his grip on Chip. "Mind your tongue, outsider. This man has insulted Lord Luis."

"Enough," Luis said sharply. He rose from his seat and approached Chip, his expression unreadable. "Pho is missing, yes. But tell me Chip, who do you blame for this?"

Chip's voice shook, but he held his ground. "I blame you. You harassed her, took what you pleased, and now that she's run away, you've left my wife and I *nothing!*"

Luis laughed. He laughed like he had just heard the funniest thing he had ever heard. And then the room fell silent. Drew felt Tenebrae's hand on his arm, a silent plea to stay calm. Lord Luis turned to the soldier.

"Release him," he ordered.

The soldier hesitated but obeyed. Chip stumbled forward, rubbing his wrist.

"Says the man who was so *desperate* for status," Lord Luis said, his voice cold and measured. "That he offered his daughter to me! Pho is beautiful, and she would have been worthy to sit by my side. But she has insulted me for the last time, and you, Chip, should understand this: slandering the crown and its representatives will not be tolerated."

Chip's eyes burned with defiance and betrayal, but he said nothing more. He cast a grateful glance at Geetie before being escorted out of the room.

"My apologies for the interruption," Lord Luis said, returning to his seat. "Now, where were we?"

Drew's mind raced. Chip's accusations had confirmed their suspicions: the Belrench soldiers were more than mere protectors. They were oppressors. And Luis, despite his polished façade, was complicit in their actions. He felt sick at what he had heard about Chip's daughter, Pho. It seemed that Luis had seen her as an object that would compliment his rule over Xudm.

"We were discussing trust," Drew said carefully. "It's clear that trust must be built not just between nations, but also between rulers and their people."

Lord Luis' lips twitched into a faint smile. "An astute observation. Perhaps you and I are not so different, Mr Saran."

The words felt like a veiled threat, and Drew could not shake the feeling that they were walking a fine line. As the conversation continued, Geetie's eyes remained fixed on the door, his determination clear. Whatever it took, he would find Chip's daughter – this man would not let another father lose their child. The group was escorted to their quarters within the manor, and Drew could not shake the feeling that their mission in Xudm had become far more dangerous than they had anticipated.

That night, Drew tossed and turned in his bed. Images of Chip's broken face and of Pho's name spat like a curse from Luis' lips, refused to leave him.

He felt the familiar heat of the runes on his arm – pulsing, alive. Then suddenly, the world slipped sideways.

***

Czmithicon stood atop the Temple of Nearth, staring out across his flooding kingdom. The waters surged from the west, torrents from the Great Southern Sea spilling across the plains and up into the valley.

"Flee!" he shouted, voice echoing across the collapsing stone. "Flee to the southern ranges!"

His people looked at him with terrified eyes. Behind him, guards knelt in the citadel, praying to the Demi-god of Weather.

"Please, our Lord," they cried. "Don't drown us!"

Czmithicon turned to his servant. "Greknam, has everyone escaped?"

"Yes, my lord... but what of you?"

"Go," Czmithicon said simply.

Greknam hesitated.

"Before you flee," said the king, lowering his voice. "Bring me the Ocean Sapphire. It must be hidden. Forever, if need be."

When Greknam returned, the jewel pulsed with light – bright blue and alive with power. It had been taken hundreds of years ago from the darkest depths of the

Sea of the Sun. Czmithicon took it and descended into the deepest vault of the Temple.

Though the temple was crumbling, two unmoving guards still stood at the entrance to the chamber: the Žuvkozok, not truly alive, nor truly dead. Carved of obsidian stone, they stood eternal.

"Guard this vault forever," said Czmithicon. "Let no one pass who is unworthy."

He placed the Ocean Sapphire on a spire of stone that rose like a stalactite from the cave floor.

"Here may you rest," he whispered. "Until the rightful one claims your power over the weather."

A thunderous wave roared down the corridor. The king turned to face it.

Stretching his arms wide, he welcomed his end.

"Ō Iōxx txitwž ituèa vcoh uaōž qxtèo!" he cried.

The water struck, blinding and wild. The vault was sealed by blue foam and thunderous white – a tomb for Nearth's final king. All sacred thrones were lost. And thus ended the reign of Czmithicon, last king of Nearth.

"You must be wondering why I showed you this," said a voice that echoed like thunder through still water.

Drew gasped, no longer inside the body of Czmithicon, but floating within the frozen moment – water hung in the air, the wave suspended mid-crash.

A figure shimmered into view, humanoid but translucent, skin and robes the colour of a storm.

"I showed you this because this is what happens when mortals gain the power of the Ocean Sapphire," he explained. "Their greed shattered the balance. The Ocean Sapphire nearly broke the world. It must never fall into unworthy hands again." He paused. "Lazarka has touched your path before. She reveals herself rarely, as do all the Demi-gods. I am Pogoda, the Demi-god of Weather."

Drew looked at Pogoda in awe. "Yes," he answered. "But Lazarka never showed herself to me before."

"She did not need to," explained Pogoda. "But I fear the quest for the Ocean Sapphire is now on the edge of a knife. Andrew Saran – you *must* find Pho. She is inherently linked with the sapphire…"

And then a great wind blew, and Drew was taken out of the time paused temple, waking up in a bed within Lord Luis' manor, the runes in his arms. Resolve hardened within him. The girl that Luis had traumatised was key to this, and now the companions finally had a clear path forward.

Chapter Twenty-Four

They rode out onto the darkening road, Pho looking in fear at the all too familiar jungle that grew on both sides of the main highway between Maṭtā and Phārā. Haunting memories of becoming lost in the rainforest, as well as being pursued by bandits, were atop her mind. She found herself holding Josh tightly as she sat behind him on the horse, his presence making her feel safe and secure. On he rode, his confidence and resoluteness radiating and filling Pho with hope. She had guarded the Ocean Sapphire for too long now to allow it to fall into the wrong hands, and she was just as determined as Josh was in finding it.

"How long did you say it was to ride from Maṭtā to Phārā again?" asked Josh, shouting above the clippity-clopping of the horse.

"Two days," answered Pho.

"I can do it in one," said Josh with determination. "Ya!"

He willed the horse onward, pushing the beast to its limits as the duo rode along the road and closer to Phārā. Eventually, night fell and the road was lit only by the crescent moon in the sky. The horse began slowing, and Josh decided that they should rest for a couple of hours.

"Agreed," yawned Pho. "I'm getting tired."

They pulled the horse off the road and into the trees. Josh made a small fire and decided to clear out underneath the roots of a nearby strangler fig. Pho was grateful that this time, Josh was here to clear out any bugs or critters from below the tree. She cringed as she remembered the last time she spent a night in the jungle.

"You can sleep there," said Josh. "It's clear of any insects or creepy crawlies. I'll sleep by the fire."

Pho nodded. "Thanks, Josh," she said.

Josh smirked at her. "What would you do without me?"

Unintentionally, his flirtatious question re-awakened those memories within Pho of when she *was* on her own in this place. Josh seemed to notice, and he apologised profusely.

"Do you want to talk about it?" he asked.

Pho shook her head. "Not yet," she said. "Perhaps when all this is over. I just want to get out of here."

Josh smiled. "I understand," he replied. "Well, rest. Don't worry about the jungle."

With that, Pho curled up under the tree. As she settled in, she heard the sound of hooves coming from the road, back through the trees. She shuddered as several horses rode past them, clearly bound for Mạttā. Josh quickly extinguished the fire, turning the world black.

"Can't be too careful," he whispered. "Especially after what you told me about the bandits that roam around here."

Despite being in the middle of the jungle – again – Pho felt safe this time. Josh made her feel comfortable and looked after, and it was a feeling that Pho enjoyed. Surprisingly, she slept well that night.

***

Rain poured upon the empty streets, and Pho felt a feeling of dread as she and Josh approached Phārā. As promised, Josh had indeed got them to Pho's home village within just over a day, far quicker than the two day estimate most gave to travel between the two villages. Josh gave Pho a cloak and she put it on, hoping to avoid being recognised and then hauled before her father and Commander Luis.

"I won't let them get you," Josh had promised. "You're safe with me. Luis won't get his hands anywhere near, you can be sure of that."

She sat in a large thick coat, a hood over her head, as their steed strode down the rainy main street of Phārā. She was shocked when she began to sweat, the warmth of the cloak greater than expected.

"They make them good in Grashnâk," explained Josh. "My great grandmother gave it to me when I visited her there, once."

Pho smiled. "Tell me more about your family," she asked.

"Well," began Josh. "My father was originally from Grashnâk, an island in the Outer Dirtgulas. But he moved to mainland Harleland and to the Central Dutchies when he was a young man. Now he's the land's most successful food merchant." He sighed. "I just hope he and the others survived. If Irk, Murk and I could, then so can they."

"I'm sure he has!" said Pho, rubbing Josh's arm. "If he's anything like you, he'd have found a way."

"I refuse to believe anything else," said Josh, though his voice trembled. He shook his head. "My father found me as a child in Canterbury."

"He must love you," replied Pho.

"He does," replied Josh.

They found a horse wandering alone near the square, a similar saddle to their own upon its back.

"This must be the horse that Irk and Murk stole," suggested Pho.

Josh nodded. They dismounted their horse, and tied both steeds up together, ready to eventually send them back to the boy in Mạttā when they got the chance.

He went to say more, but was interrupted by a Belrench soldier who had spotted the pair.

"Halt!" he called. "More strangers in Phārā?"

"More?" asked Josh. "Tell me sir, you haven't happened to see two slimy individuals with strange armour on?"

"I don't answer questions from *foreigners*!" replied the soldier, clearly insulted by Josh for simply asking.

Pho rolled her eyes. "I'm not foreign," she said. "Can I ask?"

"Why would a Xudist woman such as yourself be travelling with a foreign man?" asked the soldier. "Take that hood off so I can see who you are!"

"Answer the question first, and then I will," answered Pho.

"Fine, very well," said the soldier. "We spotted two shady fellows down by the beach earlier. It looked like they were felling the dune trees, perhaps trying to construct a boat to sail back whence they came."

"Ha!" laughed Josh. "If those two think they can sail over the Sea of Many Currents in nothing more than a DIY dinghy, they can think again." Josh looked at the soldier. "They are fugitives of ours, we are trying to round them up," he said. "They stole something of value from Harleland."

"Harleland?" asked the soldier. "Are you with the others that just left?"

"Others?" asked Josh. "From Harleland? Who!?"

"Well… Hey, no questions, remember!"

"Oh, you…" Josh rolled his eyes in frustration, and turned to Pho. "Can you handle this?"

Pho laughed. "I might be able to," she said with a smirk. She looked at the soldier. "Can you tell us about the others from Harleland?"

The soldier sighed in frustration. "All I know was that a group of them got sent up to Lord Luis' manor for questioning. I think I heard the name 'Crysthan' used for one of them."

"So they *did* survive!" shouted Josh in happiness. "I knew it!" Then his expression changed. "Crysthan…" he growled. "That traitor is still with them."

"Where did they go?" asked Pho.

"Well, they seemed to bolt out pretty early this morning," explained the soldier. "Bound for Mạttā."

Josh put his head in his hand. "That group last night!" he said. "It was probably them! We missed them!" He cried out in frustration.

Pho suddenly had another question – the way that the soldier had referred to Luis as *Lord* instead of *Commander*.

"Isn't it Commander Luis?" she asked.

"He's just been appointed by King Benjamin the Great as his Xudist vassal!" explained the soldier with pride. "He's Lord of Xudm now."

Pho's heart dropped. This was terrible. Luis would have supreme authority to do what he pleased with her now – as if he did not already have it before anyway. This just made it worse. If he decided to search for her, she would never be able to escape. She looked at Josh in terror, but he looked back in determination.

"He won't find you, Pho," he said. "That's a promise."

Chapter Twenty-Five

"Now's our chance," whispered Crysthan.

The Herk Captain had spent the night drawing up plans to escape from Lord Luis' manor, unable to rest while he was stuck as a prisoner within the walls of the Lord of Xudm's abode. Drew knew Crysthan hated the feeling of being trapped. He remembered the Herk Captain's resolve as he was tortured by King Lekt back in Wilder Forest. This was a true soldier, and with the new era of peace back home, Drew hoped that perhaps he and Crysthan could fight side by side one day. Perhaps this was that day. Crysthan's plan involved the stealing of horses from Luis' stables, while Drew had suggested finding Chip before leaving Phārā to search for the girl called Pho that Pogoda had mentioned. He hoped that her father may be able to give some clue about where she may have run away too. They had already snuck outside and stood in the darkness of the night in front of the stables.

"I can see the guards are starting to lose focus!" whispered Crysthan again, as Tenebrae began to sneak around the back of the stables.

Her task was simple – untie the horses as quietly as possible to avoid the companions being spotted. Geetie watched beside them with bated breath. His task was to help Drew find Chip. Drew knew that Geetie wanted to help Chip find his daughter, a way perhaps to help him grieve the loss of his own son. Drew gripped the hilt of his sword tightly, his eyes darting between the flickering torches carried by the patrolling guards. The night air was crisp, carrying the scent of hay and damp earth. Crysthan crouched low, his silhouette barely visible against the darkened stable walls. The Herk

Captain's breath was steady, but Drew could feel the tension radiating from him.

"Almost there," Crysthan murmured, his voice barely audible over the chirping crickets. Drew gave a small nod, glancing over at Geetie. The older man's face was etched with determination, his hands clenched into fists as if ready to spring into action at any moment. Drew had seen that look before, back when Geetie first joined them on the quest to the Great Tower. It was a look of a man trying to redeem himself.

From the corner of his eye, Drew spotted movement. Tenebrae emerged from the shadows, her lean frame blending seamlessly with the night. She gave a quick hand signal – the horses were untied. Crysthan's plan was working, at least for now. Drew felt a flicker of hope, but it was quickly tempered by the knowledge that things rarely went smoothly.

"Geetie, stay close," Drew whispered. "If things go south, we'll need to move fast."

Geetie nodded. "Let's find Chip," he suggested.

Drew knew the man's heart was heavy. Chip had become something of a lifeline for Geetie, a chance to channel his grief into something meaningful. Finding Pho would mean more than just helping Chip; it would mean giving Geetie a purpose.

Crysthan motioned for them to follow. The group moved as one, their footsteps muffled against the soft ground. The stable doors loomed ahead, slightly ajar. Drew's heart raced as he heard the muffled voices of the guards nearby. They could not afford to make a mistake now.

"Let's move," Crysthan said, his tone commanding but calm. Drew and Geetie slipped through the door, finding themselves in the stable's shadowy interior. The horses snorted softly, their large eyes reflecting the dim light. Tenebrae was already at work, guiding the animals toward the exit.

"Hurry," she hissed.

Suddenly, a sharp clink echoed through the air. Drew's stomach dropped. He turned to see Geetie's foot brushing against a loose bucket. The sound was not loud, but in the stillness of the night, it might as well have been a thunderclap.

"What was that?" a guard's voice called out.

"Stay here," Crysthan ordered. He slipped into the shadows, moving like a wraith toward the approaching footsteps. Drew held his breath, his hand on his sword, ready to spring into action if needed. Geetie looked stricken, mouthing an apology, but Drew shook his head. There was no time for blame.

The sound of a scuffle broke the silence. Drew tensed, but within moments, Crysthan reappeared, his expression grim.

"Dealt with," he said tersely. "Let's go before more show up."

As they led the horses out of the stables, Drew's thoughts turned to Chip. They could not leave Phārā without talking to him. Finding Pho was a priority if they were ever going to find the Ocean Sapphire. He glanced at Geetie, who seemed to read his mind.

"We'll find him," Geetie said firmly. "We have to."

Drew nodded, hoping that Geetie's conviction would be enough to carry them through the night.

***

"Chip?" asked the beggar, his voice echoing loudly through the alleyways of Phārā.

Drew cringed as he looked around. No soldiers in sight. He breathed a sigh of relief, as Crysthan looked at the beggar sternly.

"Please keep it down!" he pleaded. "Do you know where Chip lives?"

"I think it's the one just over there," said the beggar, pointing to a two storey house on the other side of the village square. "I think that's his anyway. Anyways, any change?"

Geetie reached into his pockets and gave the beggar some loose change. "It's Harlelish currency I'm afraid, but it's all I've got," explained Geetie.

"Thank you sir!" said the beggar. "I won't forget this!"

"Well, who's knocking on the door?" asked Crysthan.

"I am!" said Geetie with resolve. "Come on, let's go."

With that, the company left the beggar in the alleyway and crossed the village square towards the house he had pointed out. Geetie approached the front door and knocked. A few seconds went by. Silence. Drew breathed in apprehension. And then it was opened a crack, a man suspiciously peeking out.

"What do you want at this time of night?" he asked hastily.

"Chip?" asked Geetie.

"Yes!" said the man. "What do you *want?!* Unless it's about my daughter you can bugger off!"

"It is about her!" said Geetie quickly. "We need your help to find her."

The door opened and Chip stepped out.

"You?" he said. "The ones that Luis dragged up to his manor yesterday?"

Geetie nodded. "Indeed we are."

He introduced the companions and explained the situation. Chip watched on in confusion as Drew told him about the Ocean Sapphire.

"I remember Luis giving her a beautiful, glowing blue jewel just before she ran away," he explained. "Are you seriously telling me that that was some sort of mystical, magic object?"

"Well," said Drew. "Yes."

Chip scowled. "You foreign *troublemakers* are just here to gloat! Enough of this hocus pocus Ocean Sapphire nonsense! I just want my daughter back!"

"Actually," said a voice from behind Chip. "I think they're right about the jewel."

"Thu?" asked Chip, turning to his wife behind him. "Don't tell me *you* believe this nonsense too!?"

"I saw it!" explained Thu. "I was helping Pho in her room, maybe two days before she ran away... she left me alone in there for maybe a minute, but... the blue orb started going crazy! And I heard voices – both good and evil." She paused, looking at Drew and his friends in horror. "It was like they were fighting each other!"

Drew stared back, wide eyed. He turned quickly to Tenebrae. "The evil voice I heard... do you think he could talk to me because he hijacked the runes I carried?"

"Perhaps Pogoda was able to fight the voice off from taking over the Weather Runes," suggested Tenebrae, looking thoughtful.

Drew nodded and then turned back to Chip and Thu. "It is imperative we find your daughter," he announced. "Both for your sake and perhaps even for the sake of the world."

Chip looked downcast. "I just..." he muttered. "I can only think of one place she could have run off too. Her sister's place, although that is in Maṭṭā, and I can't imagine her chance of survival if she travelled there alone."

"Then that is where we need to start looking," declared Geetie with determination.

"I will come with you," said Chip. "I can't continue to sit here. I must find Pho!"

"So be it," said Drew. "We shall set out at once!"

Chapter Twenty-Six

Josh and Pho raced toward the beach. It was imperative they found Irk and Murk before they had a chance to escape back to the Crownlands with the Ocean Sapphire. There was no sign of the Herks, however Josh suggested that they split up and search the dunes. Pho raced up the sandy slopes, ignoring the scratching of sharp sticks and thorns from the dune plants, desperate to find the jewel before it was too late. After everything she had been through with the Ocean Sapphire, she could not let it be stolen now. Nothing in the trees immediately stood out to her, however after a few minutes Pho came across felled branches and piles of bark. Someone had clearly been cutting down the trees and using this area to craft something.

"Josh!" she called. "I think I've found where they were building their boats."

Josh ran over from farther in the forest. He looked at the site in frustration.

"And now those two good-for-nothing Herks are nowhere to be seen!" he said, irritation clearly etched on his face.

Pho scanned the immediate area. There were clear tracks left by someone – or something being dragged. Two things being dragged. However the tracks stopped near the bottom of the sand dunes. Pho considered whether the waves had washed the tracks away, however the sand was dry, and she knew the tide never rose that high.

"I don't think they made it to the water," she said, indicating the tracks to Josh.

Josh nodded in interest. "Maybe they realised that their crappy little boats would never have made it back over the sea," he suggested.

Pho laughed. She certainly enjoyed Josh's company. He continued to try and make light of their current dire situation. It was a welcome change to the sombre mood of the past few weeks.

"So if Irk and Murk didn't end up trying to cross the sea," began Pho. "Then where did they go?"

"Over there! Look!"

Pho and Josh whipped around. To her horror, she recognised some of Commander Luis' right hand men not far away through the trees. Her heart dropped.

"It's Pho!" cried one of them.

"Josh, we need to run!" she cried.

"Too where?" asked Josh. "Into the sea? Face it Pho, we've been caught."

"Pho," said the patrol leader. "Our Lord has been missing you."

"Stay away from her!" warned Josh, placing a hand on his sword hilt.

The accompanying soldiers moved around Josh, greatly outnumbering him. The leader smiled.

"You are both under arrest," he explained gleefully. "Follow me."

Reluctantly, they followed, Pho's heart dropping even further when she realised her and Josh were being shepherded straight toward Luis' manor.

Pho looked over at Josh. He had promised to protect her from Luis. He had told her he would not let him get her. Yet here they both were, in rope bonds, being dragged toward the man who had ruined Pho's life. Josh's head was down, his confidence clearly gone. He looked over at her, clearly feeling her gaze on him.

"I'm sorry," he whispered.

"That's enough!" called the soldier who walked behind Josh.

Josh said no more and continued to walk forward. Soon, Luis' manor could be seen, the majestic mansion towering over the outskirts of Phārā. After another few moments, they were before the doors. Although Luis had been courting Pho for quite some time, she had never actually been inside his manor. It was incredible. There was a small feeling telling Pho that living in a place like this may not be so bad. But she pushed it away. She would be living in a beautiful cage if she agreed to marry Luis just to reside in this majestic mansion. The doors opened and the group stepped through. Pho's blood turned cold. There he was, standing before them. Commander Luis. Now known as *Lord* Luis, ruler of Xudm on behalf of the Belrench King.

"My love!" he called, his eyes fixing themselves on Pho. "I have worried for you night and day!" He put his hand on his head dramatically. Pho was unsure if he was exaggerating on purpose. "Sleep has not come to me in so long, my sweet! I have sent out patrols of men to find you, but alas, for they were all unable to locate my beautiful bride-to-be!"

He signalled for them to enter, the doors closing behind them as the group stepped into the entrance hall. Flames flickered on torches, and rich tapestries decorated the walls. Luis stopped just before the stairs which led to the upper levels of his manor. He looked at Josh, his eyes narrowing.

"And who have we here?" Luis asked. "Another Harlelish diplomat here to discuss trade?"

"Where are my friends?" asked Josh in a no nonsense tone.

"Well this one seems to be on guard," chided Luis. "Your friends appear to have left. I gave them the courtesy of staying in my humble abode, but alas, they ran off late last night."

"I don't blame them for wanting to get away from a creep like you," replied Josh in spite.

Luis laughed. "A brave man is he who questions a Lord in his own house," he said. Then, his tone changed. Anger came across his face. "But I warn you, *boy*. Speak to me like that again, and I'll have your tongue. Do you understand?"

Josh stared back in silent defiance.

"I said," continued Luis. "*Do you understand!?*"

"Perfectly," replied Josh, anger etched on his face.

"Good," said Luis. "General!" He called over the leader of the patrol that had found them in the forest by the beach earlier. "Report. What were these two up to?"

"We found them checking out the same area where those other two dingbats had been trying to build boats earlier," the General explained.

"Ah, I see," said Luis. "So Harleland and the Crownlands think they can take their Civil War over to Xudm do they?" He clicked his fingers. To Pho's surprise, two soldiers came downstairs into the hall, Irk and Murk in their stead, their hands tied.

"Irk and Murk here have been most helpful," Luis snickered.

"You two *traitors*!" cried Josh. "What have you done with the…" he trailed off, careful not to namedrop the Ocean Sapphire in front of Luis. But to Pho's horror, Luis' grin only widened, and he withdrew the blue, glowing orb from his robes.

"…this?" asked Luis. "What have you done with *this* is what you were meant to say, hmm?"

"Hand that over!" cried Josh.

"Oh, I think I'll keep this actually," said Luis. "After all, it is not everyday someone comes across *the runes*."

"I'm warning you!" yelled Josh, but Luis flicked his hand in dismissal.

"Take him away," he commanded.

Luis' minions grabbed at Josh, the young Protector continuing to yell warnings and curses at Luis as he was taken to some prison that Pho did not want to think about.

"It's for your own good!" he yelled. "When Drew finds you, you're finished if you don't give that back!"

Luis shrugged. Josh was taken through some doors behind the stairs and his cries were cut off as they closed with a *clang!* Pho gulped. Luis looked upon her.

"You have betrayed me, my love," he said. "Guards! Send out a search party for this 'Drew' that he spoke of!"

"Yes, sir!" replied a soldier. He and two others ran from the manor to begin their mission.

Luis stepped closer. He knelt down in front of Pho and held the Ocean Sapphire to her face.

"How lucky it was that you and that boy found this," he said.

"His name is Hax!" said Pho in anger.

"Oh, yes that's right. I don't care." Luis turned to Irk and Murk. "Tell me more about this Drew," he commanded. "Why is he and these Harlelish invaders looking for runes?"

"His full name is Andrew Saran, milord," replied Irk. "He's descended from some Demi-god from ages ago. I think he already has two sets of runes."

Luis seemed to ponder the information. "Two sets, eh?" he said. "And this sapphire here – you told me earlier it contains the Weather Runes – would be his third set?"

"That's right," said Murk.

"Tell me, my dear Herks," said Luis. "Do you like money?"

Irk and Murk both nodded their heads enthusiastically.

"Good," replied Luis with a smirk. "Find this Saran. Convince him to come back to me here. Tell him that I shall help him find the Ocean Sapphire. If you need, kill those soldiers I already sent. I can always find more anyway. I shall pay you twenty thousand Brancs each."

Irk and Murk's eyes lit up. "Brancs?" Irk said in excitement. "But one Branc is worth, like, ten Crowns back home!"

"We'll be richer than Count Michael!" crowed Murk. "Of course, Lord Luis! We'll do it."

"Very well," replied Luis. "Release them!"

At his command, the guards released the two Herks, setting them loose on their mission to find Drew. Irk and Murk left the manor, leaving Pho alone with Luis and the two guards.

"Now then, Pho," said Luis. "Let's have a little talk about our future."

Pho gulped.

Chapter Twenty-Seven

Drew was exhausted. He had not had a proper night's sleep since before they had landed on the vanishing island, days ago. Since they had arrived in Xudm, it had been non-stop. Now he, Tenebrae, Geetie, Crysthan and Chip had arrived in the village of Mạttā, where Pho had supposedly run away too.

"I'll take you straight to my daughters' house," said Chip, leading the way. "I haven't seen her in over a year." He sighed. "At least that's one positive thing about this situation."

Tenebrae smiled. "I can't wait to meet her," she said. "You said she's called Ara, right?"

"That's right," replied Chip. "I remember before she left home, she always used to knit the prettiest throw blankets I have ever seen." A tear formed in his eye. He shook his head. "I wonder if she has made any more in the past year."

"That's lovely," said Tenebrae. "She must be very talented."

"She is," replied Chip. "They both are, her and Pho. Pho has the most incredible shell collection, so I suggested to her to start selling them at the local market each Sunday." He sobbed. "If I see her again, I'll tell her I love her."

Drew walked on, trying not to show the emotions within him after listening to Chip and Tenebrae's conversation. Although he struggled to contain himself, he still had a sense of wanting to keep his gruff exterior. Drew had dropped back behind the group. Tears rushed down his face. The reality of losing Josh was beginning to set in, coupled with his exhaustion and the impending death of Octavia.

"Drew?" asked Geetie, putting a hand on his shoulder. "It's alright, son."

"I'm sorry," sobbed Drew. "Must be my allergies."

Geetie shook his head. "Some allergies," he said, rolling his eyes. "Let's just get that sapphire and then get out of here. We're so close now."

Drew nodded. "You're right. Let's finish this."

Drew sighed. He was failing to protect his friends. If Josh was dead and Octavia was dying, who was next? He felt sick as he imagined Tenebrae skewered by a Belrench soldier, or Geetie decapitated by a Herk. It was just them three now, unless by some miracle Octavia still lived.

"Here we are!" called Chip.

The company now stood before a small yet humble house, tucked away in a side street near the village square. Chip knocked. A few moments passed. Then, the door opened, and a young woman stepped out.

"Father!?" she called.

"Oh, Ara!" called Chip, as he embraced his eldest daughter. "And is Pho here, too?"

Ara shook her head. "She went after those thieves," she explained. "They stole something of value. A blue jewel."

Drew's heart dropped. "What!?" he screeched. "Who stole it?"

"They were with this young man... Josh his name was," she explained.

"Josh!" yelled Geetie in joy. "He's *alive!*"

Drew was ecstatic! He felt happiness course through him, the like of which he had not felt in a long time, as he embraced Geetie and Tenebrae.

"Who are these people?" asked Ara. "They wear the same clothes as Josh did."

As Chip explained to Ara, Crysthan turned to Drew.

"Irk and Murk," said Crysthan darkly. "They stole it on Grand Duke Shârvous' orders."

"Well we must find them," said Geetie. "And Josh, too! Perhaps he'll know where they've run off too."

"Pho and Josh went together, tracking them down," explained Ara.

Drew nodded. "Come on then, no time to lose!" he commanded.

"I'm going to stay here, with my Ara," said Chip. "Please bring Pho back safely."

"I promise you, I'll do whatever I can," said Drew. "That's what Protectors do."

"I'm going to find my boy," said Geetie with determination. "Let's waste no more time here."

With that, the company of Drew, Geetie, Tenebrae and Crysthan set out once more. Drew turned to the Herk Captain, wishing to know more about Shârvous' orders.

"I think you have some explaining to do," he said.

Crysthan nodded. "After you defeated me back in Wilder Forest, I was hauled before my Lord, and your uncle. He sent me on a mission to follow you, to try and steal the next set of runes from you." He sighed. "But after what we've been through since we snuck aboard that ship, I realised… I can't complete that mission anymore. Lord Shârvous was acting on advice from Count Michael. I can't serve Count Michael anymore."

Drew acknowledged the Captain's words. "You will be a very welcome member of the Protectors back in Harleland," he said.

"I appreciate the gesture," said Crysthan. "But I'm still in love with the Crownlands. I still have affections for Lord Shârvous. However I know how he operates. He will not be pleased when he learns of what I've done to help you."

"Well, you'll still be welcome," said Drew. "And we'll do whatever we can to bring peace to both Harleland and the Crownlands."

Crysthan nodded.

"Now," continued Drew. "If we can find Irk and Murk, you can command them to hand the Ocean Sapphire back over."

Drew pondered how strange it was to befriend a Herk of the Crownlands, and a Captain no less. His heart ached as he remembered Kora, the first girl he had ever loved, brutally cut down by Shârvous' men over a year ago. He had hated Herks before, but after that, he had sworn to slay them all. His hatred of the Crownlands knew no bounds. He was much more level headed nowadays, and he knew now that there were good Herks like Crysthan. Everything was not black and white, and it was a lesson Drew had learned over the past several months.

"Right on que," said Tenebrae, snapping Drew from his thoughts.

He whipped around. To Drew's complete and utter shock, Irk and Murk stalked out from behind a small hut, their hands in the air.

"It's just us!" called Irk.

"At last," said Crysthan. "Do you have the sapphire?"

"Well–" began Murk, but suddenly Geetie interrupted them.

"Where is my son?" asked Geetie anxiously.

"The sapphire was taken from us," said Murk quickly, as Irk tried to recoil back from Geetie.

"Josh is safe," he said. "Please, just hear us out!"

"Taken?" asked Crysthan. "By who!"

"It got taken by some shady figure," said Murk. "But we met someone who can help."

Irk nodded. "Lord Luis himself told us he is willing to help find the Ocean Sapphire."

Drew turned to his friends, a look of annoyance plastered on his face. "Luis," he sighed, rolling his eyes.

"Back to Phārā then, huh?" said Tenebrae.

"It appears so," said Drew. "Alright you two – take us to Luis."

"Of course!" said Irk.

"Yeah!" echoed Murk. "We're all friends!"

Drew and Geetie exchanged a glance. Geetie shrugged. "I can be friends with anyone," he said.

"Oi, what's all this racket?" called a Belrench soldier, who had rounded the corner and was walking towards them.

"Time to go," suggested Crysthan.

"Agreed," said Geetie. "Ho, soldier! Sorry, big night for us. We'll keep it down!"

"You better!" warned the soldier, walking back around the corner.

"Okay, let's get back to the horses and get out of here," said Drew.

So it was that the company began the journey back to Phārā. And Drew knew that this time, things were about to reach a head.

Chapter Twenty-Eight

"The game's up Luis," said Pho, staring at the Lord of Xudm in defiance.

Luis sighed. "Very well," he admitted. "Since you won't be leaving this place again, I suppose I can let you in on a secret."

Pho felt sick at his words. Luis continued.

"When we were to be married, I never intended to give your father – Chad, was it? – the status that he craved," he said. "But it seems like that was obvious to you for a while." He snickered, clearly pleased with himself.

"Oh, it was obvious alright," said Pho. "And having me around as an object was obvious too."

She surprised herself at her confidence in talking back to Luis, but her feeling of being backed into a corner outweighed her usual passive self.

Luis shrugged. "I'm just a man," he said. "But you're not the only beautiful woman who lives in Xudm, and rest assured, I have all my options lined up."

"So what happens to me now?" asked Pho. "If you won't let me leave, am I to become your maid or something?"

"I haven't thought that far ahead to be honest," admitted Luis. "It's not important. *You're* not important." He grinned. "My only priority right now is meeting this Drew Saran figure. The power he holds intrigues me."

"You're already the Lord of Xudm," said Pho, her anger rising. "What more do you want?"

"With the runes, I could achieve supernatural power!" said Luis. He dropped his voice to a whisper. "I could even take the throne of Belrance from King Ben! And then expand our Kingdom to rival the Augustines as Nearth's next great Empire!"

"You're mad," spat Pho.

"I call it ambitious," replied Luis. He shrugged. "You could have been Queen of Nearth if you had married me."

"And here's the thing you forget about *ordinary* people, Luis," said Pho. "Or the people you see as 'lower class peasants'. People like me don't want or need power. We just want to live simple and peaceful lives. Surrounded by friends and family. Not by empty, soulless mansions and minions, and certainly not by magic runes."

"Then you lack vision," replied Luis, a hint of anger in his voice. "I don't need to justify myself to you!" He stood up. "Guards! Take her away!"

Luis' minions grabbed roughly at Pho's arms and dragged her out of the hall. Soon, they were walking down a flight of stone stairs, heading into the dungeons below Luis' manor. The soldiers – two of them – yanked her down, her feet slipping on the stone stairs and her arm being twisted by one of the guards. Eventually, they reached the bottom of the stairwell and Pho was thrown into a waiting cell. The guards laughed and then turned and walked back upstairs.

"Pho!" called a familiar voice. "Is it really you?"

Pho shook her head. Josh? No. She did not expect Luis to keep her and Josh together. No, this was the voice of none other than Hax!

"Hax!" she called. "How are you here?"

She gasped as the boy approached her. He looked malnourished and dirty, like he had not been fed for days.

"Luis got his goons to throw me in here," he croaked. "I think he just forgot about me though, because I haven't been given food or even water in about three days."

Pho knelt down to tend to the boy. Her hatred of Luis was now at an unimaginable level. The cruelty this man had shown knew no bounds.

"Luis said he moved you and your mother to another village," she said.

"Well, he was half right," explained Hax. "He moved my mum to a village called Beitâ. But, me…" he trailed off. "He threw me in here to 'teach me a lesson', apparently."

"We have to escape from here, Hax," said Pho. "We need to get out of here, rescue Josh – he's a friend, he can help us – and then find the rightful owner of the Ocean Sapphire."

"Ocean Sapphire?" asked Hax. "Is that what the Sajak I found is called?"

Pho nodded. "And if we can help get it to its rightful owner, then he can defeat Luis and liberate us all."

Life seemed to return to Hax's eyes. "Okay!" he said. "I'm in! But, I've looked all over this darn cell. There's nothing in here we can use to bust out."

Pho thought. She looked up at the far wall. A small window allowed a small amount of light to filter in. She realised that if the two rusty metal bars that prevented escape through the window were bent back, Hax would be small enough to slip through.

"What if we used a rock or something to bend those bars up there?" she suggested, indicating the window to Hax.

"I thought about that," said Hax. "But it's so high! I'd never be able to make it up there."

"Well you have me now, right?" said Pho. "I can lift you up there, and then you can use one of these loose rocks on the ground to bang against the bars!"

"Will you be able to lift me for that long?" asked Hax, clearly unsure.

Pho looked at him with determination. "I'll have too," she said. "Because if I can't, then we're stuck here. Probably for the rest of our lives. And I refuse to spend my last few days in Luis' cell."

"Fine," said Hax. "Let's try it."

"We'll have to choose a moment when those guards aren't gonna come down," suggested Pho. "How often do they come down here?"

"Never," replied Hax glumly. "Maybe if they did, they'd see I haven't been fed in days."

Pho looked at the boy in sadness. He was so young to have to go through torment such as this. She knew he would carry the emotional scars of this ordeal for the rest of his life. Not for the first time, she cursed Luis and the Belrench occupiers.

"Okay, let's move," she said.

Pho helped Hax to climb up onto her shoulders. The boy was not heavy, and Pho did not seem to have much difficulty in keeping him up. Hax managed to grab onto one of the bars with his right hand, a loose rock from the floor of the cell in his left hand. He began to hammer at the first bar, Pho cringing at the sound of clanging. She prayed the noise would not travel upstairs and alert the guards, but she was hopeful that they were deep enough beneath Luis' manor that no one would hear.

After a few minutes, Hax sighed in exhaustion. "It's barely made a dent," he said, sounding defeated. "But it looks so nice outside! The sun is shining, and I can smell fresh air." He dropped his head. "I just wanna get out of here…"

"We will get out of here!" said Pho. "I know it. Take a quick break, and then keep trying."

Hax took a few moments, and then returned to hammering the bar. Finally, after almost fifteen minutes of clanging and momentary rest breaks, Hax cried out in happiness.

"I've done it!" he said in excitement. "The first bar is bent right back!"

"Good job!" said Pho, starting to struggle under the constant weight of Hax. He had been standing on her shoulders now for over twenty minutes, and she was starting to feel it.

"Now onto the other one…" the boy said glumly.

He clung onto the bent bar and went to work on the other, attempting to bend it, too. Pho felt hope course through her. The plan was working. Soon, Hax would have bent both bars and made a wide enough gap for him to slip through. Then it was a matter of finding Drew, who could help save her and Josh, and ultimately defeat Luis. But at that moment, footsteps could be heard descending the stairs. Pho looked up at Hax sharply.

"Someone's coming, get down, quick!" she called in a low but urgent tone.

Hax immediately stopped what he was doing and climbed down from Pho, throwing the rock away and putting a blank expression on his face. Pho looked past the bars at the stairs and saw the figure of Lord Luis come into view.

"Ah, Pho!" he said. "I hope you are enjoying the company I gave you? I know how close you two are!"

Pho stared back at him. "You're disgusting!" she cried. "Seperating a child from his mother, and then throwing him in here? And for what? Because he comes from a lower class than you?"

"There's an order to things Pho, and you know it," said Luis. He sighed. "I grew up in a wealthy household back in mainland Belrance," he explained. "My father was President of my city's fencing club, and we had members ranging from the Lord Mayor to our local representative to the King. It would be a dishonour to associate with anyone from below that elite class."

Pho shook her head. In some ways, this was just the way Luis was raised. She understood that. But she also understood that everyone had the ability to learn and understand other perspectives and other people.

"You've had plenty of time to learn and change since you were posted to Xudm," she replied. "And you haven't. I'm judging you on that, not on your upbringing."

Luis scoffed. "So be it," he said, waving his hand at her dismissively.

He clicked his fingers, and from up the stairs, a servant came down carrying two dishes.

"Consider this as today's daily meal," he said.

Luis turned and walked back up, the servant pushing the dishes under the bars. Hax ran over and began to eat and drink, woofing down his meal like a starved animal.

"I never thought I'd see food or water again!" he cried happily.

Pho smiled. She was happy that Hax finally had something to fill him up. She looked at her own meal. It was the same as Hax's, some leftover slop that Luis' personal chef had set aside for the dogs. She decided not to smell it, lest it remove her appetite. She knew food would be few and far between in this place, so she forced herself to eat. She also shuddered in relief. Luis had not seen the bent bar on the high window. Their route to escape was still open to them.

Chapter Twenty-Nine

"We need to check your identification please."

The Belrench soldiers before them seemed to be encroaching on the company, as Drew felt for his sword hilt. Tenebrae shuffled on her horse beside him, her hand also on her knife, ready to fight if needed.

"I've told you already," said Drew. "We are here on a diplomatic mission from Harleland. We spoke to your Lord earlier, and now we are seeking adequate places within the village to set up an embassy."

That last part was of course a lie. Drew needed to buy them time to find Pho, Josh and the Ocean Sapphire so they could get out of this place and return home.

"You shall go no farther into Phārā," commanded the lead soldier. "In fact, you'll be coming with us straight back to Lord Luis' manor."

"Oh I don't think so," said Geetie. "We've already been there and hated it, thanks."

The soldier unsheathed his sword, his companions following suit. "I wasn't asking," he said ominously.

"If we're going to fight," said Crysthan. "Let us do it away from the village so the civilians don't get hurt."

Drew nodded. "Or we can avoid fighting altogether, if only you would all just listen to me."

The Belrench commander scoffed. "I have listened to you," he said. "But my decision is still that you are to come back to our Lord's abode."

Drew turned to the others. "It's not worth fighting over," he said. "Especially in the middle of the village."

Tenebrae nodded. "I agree," she said. "As much as I don't want to go back to Luis'."

"At last, some sense," said the commander. "Follow."

Drew and the others reluctantly followed the Belrench soldiers through the streets of Phārā. Drew noticed that a crowd of people were assembling near the edge of town. His heart dropped when he saw a guillotine in the middle of the crowd. Someone was set to be put to death.

They passed the guillotine and rode now upon a well-tended lawn toward the majestic mansion of Lord Luis. Suddenly, an unexpected battle cry rang out.

"Wait, stop!" cried Crysthan, but it was too late.

Irk and Murk charged forward together into the Belrench soldiers, taking them by surprise. Four of the five soldiers lay dead, a fifth charging off back into the village.

"What in the…?" asked Crysthan. "What have you *done!?*"

"Sorry, sir," said Irk. "But we want all the credit for ourselves, not for some Belrench swine."

"Credit?" asked Tenebrae. "What do you mean? What game have you two runts been playing?"

Irk snickered as Murk rode up to the manor doors. Irk looked at Drew.

"He promised us money if we gave him you," he said.

Drew scowled. His hatred of the Herks, dormant for sometime, came out. He unsheathed his blade and lunged at Irk.

"Drew, stop!" cried Geetie, but it was too late.

Drew and Irk had become locked in a battle. He looked over the Herk in disdain. He remembered the raids on the orphanage back in Dempair when he was younger, the murder of Kora, the way that Captain Dirk had hunted them relentlessly on the journey to the Great Tower. He remembered the assassination of his father at the hands of the aforementioned Captain, under orders from his uncle, Count Michael. He wondered why he ever put this anger aside. He had become soft.

Blinded by rage, Drew attempted to strike Irk to kill. The Herk expertly dodged, and then bore his own blade down onto Drew. He quickly positioned his sword to block, before the pair began to parry. Irk sidestepped and tried to uppercut Drew, but he jumped back and elbowed Irk in the side. The Herk cried out in pain before trying swing his blade around to cut at Drew's arm. Tenebrae, Geetie and Crysthan raced over to intervene, but it was too dangerous, lest they be injured or worse. Geetie and Tenebrae looked at Drew in horror, while Crysthan stared at him with an unreadable expression. By now, Drew was tiring, as was Irk, and their blows started to become clumsier each strike. Then, just as

Drew and Irk went to trade blows once more, a commanding voice spoke up.

"Halt!" it said.

Drew did not hear, and his blade clashed with Irk's, before he felt himself being detained. He swung his sword around wildly before he felt himself being thrown to the ground. He looked around in anger. He was being held down by Belrench soldiers, while before him, Lord Luis and Murk stood together on the lawn.

"An exquisite battle, Mr Saran," said Luis. "But I'd rather my lawn not get anymore blood on it." He looked at the bodies of his soldiers in distaste. Drew got up from the ground, wincing from his wounds. "Now, something I've learned since our last meeting is that you carry some rather interesting objects."

Drew looked ahead at the Ruler of Xudm. He knew what Luis was about to say next. Irk and Murk had spilled his secrets to him.

"I'd like to re-start our trade negotiations," continued Luis. "Hand me the Shadow and Life Runes! And I shall hand you over your friend Josh."

"Never!" spat Drew.

Geetie instinctively shot his hand out to quiet Drew's outburst. His face was a mask of conflict. Drew could see the battle waging within him, love of his son warring with his understanding that Luis must not get these runes.

"How do we know you actually have Josh?" asked Drew, looking at Luis suspiciously.

"Oh, I took the liberty of organising his public execution for you," replied Luis.

Drew's heart dropped. The guillotine they had rode past earlier! Geetie immediately turned tail and sped off towards the execution site. Luis looked at Drew with a huge grin.

"So, Andrew Saran," he said coldly. "What will it be? Keep your runes and watch your friend die, and his father never forgive you? Or hand them to me, and I shall let you all go freely back to Harleland."

That was when the voice returned. Drew had not heard it for a long time, but there was no mistake.

Use the ultimate Shadow Rune, Saran! it commanded. *Say Moarte!*

Drew closed his eyes. *No!* He replied. The battle within his mind raged. He looked up and saw a horrible, swirling dark mass, fire billowing within it. A pair of red, fiery eyes glared at him.

"You will listen to me!" it said.

"Who are you?" asked Drew.

"I am the darkness that you see when you close your eyes," the thing explained. "The terror that chills your heart when you think of *death*."

Drew stood coldly in realisation.

"Four sets of runes!" the thing's voice boomed. "Four Demi-gods!"

Saran, wielder of shadows.

Lazarka, bringer of life.

Pogoda, master of weather.

"And Jer-d, bringer of *death!*"

Before Drew, five small bones appeared, a rune marking in each. These were the Death Runes, and they were being held by Jer-d himself, the Demi-god of Death. Jer-d had been speaking to him this whole time, ever since he received the Shadow Runes from King Lakton all the way back in Boron Nigh, before the quest to the Great Tower had even begun.

"What do you want?" yelled Drew over the ever increasing noise.

"I want to return!" he boomed. "I can give you so much power, Drew! You could surpass the strength of my brother, your distant ancestor! You just have to say it – *Moarte!* Rip Lord Luis apart! Just like you did to those Herks back in Hoonth!"

"Ker Gorûn mentioned you, when I got to the Great Tower," said Drew.

"A weak man!" screamed Jer-d in anger. "I offered him the same as you when I sensed a similar level of anger in his heart. But the old fool turned me down. He paid for it by being cooped up in that tower for years!"

What was he to do? The anger that had overtaken him while he fought Irk had clearly opened a passage for Jer-d's return. And the temptation gnawed at him. He could keep the runes, obtain the Ocean Sapphire, rescue Josh, go home, and save Octavia. It could all work out! All he had to do was use the ultimate Shadow Rune once more. He did once – he could do it again. Drew stared coldly at Jer-d.

"I shall do it," he said, the conflict almost tearing him apart.

"Excellent," said Jer-d. "Consider this the start of our new agreement."

Drew's eyes flew open and he stared at Lord Luis before him. From his pocket, Luis withdrew a blue, glowing orb. Drew knew what it was immediately.

"Irk and Murk were only too kind to hand this to me," explained Luis. "Let's see how it works."

He held the sapphire high above his head, and immediately storm clouds began to close in around them. The final battle was about to begin.

Chapter Thirty

"It's open!" cried Hax in excitement.

Sure enough, both bars blocking the small window had been bent back by the boy. He hoisted himself up through the window and crawled out. He turned and stuck his head back through to look down at Pho. She looked up at him in return.

"Okay, remember the plan," she said. "We need to find Andrew Saran. Tell him everything that I've told you – about the Ocean Sapphire, Luis, and Josh being held captive somewhere in here too."

Hax nodded in understanding. "I won't let you down!" he called. "Don't worry, you'll be out of here before long."

With that, the boy got up and ran off on his task. Pho slumped against the wall of the cell, sliding down and eventually sitting upon the floor. She sighed. She hoped Hax would be okay, and would not run into any trouble. She also hoped he would not take too long. She was not interested in sticking around in this awful prison for much longer, and she was concerned about a guard coming down to check on them. What would happen when they noticed Hax was missing? She knew they had not checked on Hax in days, but the prospect still worried her. She was alone in the dim light of the cell, her thoughts racing. The chill of the stone walls pressed against her back, but it was the weight of worry that truly made her shiver. Every minute that passed felt like an hour. She pressed her ear to the iron bars, listening for footsteps – a guard's approach, or perhaps the distant sound of Hax returning with help.

Instead, silence.

She rubbed her hands together, trying to fight the rising dread. The name echoed in her mind like a mantra: Andrew Saran. She hadn't even met the man, but her fate now depended on him. Could Hax really find him in time? Could he evade the guards? And if he did find Drew – would he even believe the boy?

Pho let out a long, slow breath and sank back to the floor.

"Come on, Hax," she whispered. "Please hurry."

***

Andrew Saran stared down Lord Luis. He held all five Shadow Runes in his left hand, while Luis held the Ocean Sapphire above his head, the storm clouds racing in. Lightning struck nearby, but Luis did not flinch. Drew observed the power extruding from the sapphire was beginning to run down Luis' arm. He was being overcome with energy, and seemed unaffected and unafraid of the violent storm he had summoned. Despite Drew having accepted Jer-d's offer, something within him tried to resist. He thought of Josh. The time he used *Moarte* in front of him to obliterate those Herks in Hoonth. He remembered his face. However try as he might, the temptation was too great.

"Kill me, and Josh dies!" screamed Luis above the storm. "Don't think I don't know what the runes are capable of! I have studied in the great libraries of Belrance. If you use the runes on me, then my final order to my executioner is to drop the guillotine!"

Drew hesitated. Quickly, he reached into his rune bag and withdrew the *See* rune. Casting it, he looked over Luis' mind. The Ruler of Xudm was not lying. He cast his mind to the guillotine. Sure enough, Josh was there, his head shoved into the contraption, the executioner standing by for the order. Geetie, Tenebrae and Crysthan struggled against the guards, unable to rescue Josh. He called out to his father in terror, however Geetie was powerless. Luis had Drew cornered. Even if he listened to Jer-d and wiped Luis from existence with *Moarte*, Josh would be killed and Geetie would never forgive him. Drew was about to make the most difficult decision of his life. Despite his darkening heart thanks to Jer-d, he still cared for his friends. Drew backed down.

"You win," he admitted.

Luis looked upon Drew in glee. "A wise choice, Mr Saran. This is where the legend of the Occitanie dynasty begins!" He put the Ocean Sapphire back in his pocket, and the storm overhead dissipated. "Follow! You shall hand over your runes in a grovelling display in front of the crowd by the guillotine!"

"Very well," said Drew.

He followed the soon-to-be Emperor of Nearth back towards the village, eventually reaching the edge of the crowd.

"Make way, make way!" commanded Lord Luis. "We shall have a ceremony to mark the beginning of a new order in Xudm, Belrance and the wider world of Nearth!"

"Sir," asked one of the Belrench soldiers. "What of the prisoner?"

He indicated to Josh. Luis shrugged. "Release him once the runes are handed over to me," he said. "Any funny business however and execute him immediately."

Drew noticed in the corner of his eye a young boy talking with Tenebrae. They exchanged a few words and then ran off together into the crowd, before running off towards Luis' manor. Drew had no time to follow Tenebrae, instead having to deal with the situation at hand.

"Now is the time!" yelled Luis to the assembled crowd.

Drew noticed Thu watching on, Pho's mother, while the homeless man they had run into the other night near the village square looked on at Luis' display in fear.

"A new Global Empire will rise! I, Lord Luis, shall control the Shadow, Life and Weather Runes, and shall henceforth be known as Emperor Occitanie the Great!" He turned to Drew. "You! Saran! Hand over the Shadow and Life Runes!"

Drew did as he was told, much to Josh's bewilderment.

"Drew! No!" he cried. "Don't worry about me! My death means nothing! The fate of the world is at stake now!"

He was slapped across the face by the executioner, however Josh continued to curse. Luis withdrew the Ocean Sapphire and smashed it on the ground. It broke evenly into five pieces, each shard of sapphire inscribed with a rune. They read as follows:

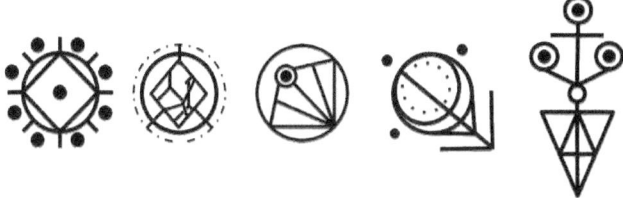

"What have you done..." asked Josh, looking at Drew in disbelief.

Drew smiled. "All for the betterment of the world," he said.

Fifteen runes were piled in Luis' cupped hands. He stared at them greedily.

"Um..." said the executioner. "Should I release him now, my Lord?"

"Sure, I don't care," answered Luis, not bothering to look at the executioner.

The executioner unbound Josh's bonds and pushed him towards Drew. Immediately, Josh went to attack Luis, however Drew held him back.

"Wait!" he said. "This is what is meant to happen."

"What do you mean?" asked Josh. He looked at Drew in anger. "You've given away all your runes to a power hungry freak!"

"You don't think I used the runes beforehand?" asked Drew.

"Wait…" said Josh. "You mean…"

"I used the *See* rune," explained Drew. "I know exactly what is about to happen."

"Get back here, you!" called a guard.

As Drew had expected, a young woman, around the same age as Josh, had busted through the crowd. She took Luis unawares, kicking him. Luis gave a cry of shock as he spilled the runes all over the ground. Drew nodded at Josh.

"Now," he commanded.

Josh ran at Luis and sliced at him. Luis did not have time to prepare himself for the assault, and he fell backward into the guillotine, causing the blade to fall, cutting his head clean off. The short reign of Emperor Occitanie the Great was over. The crowd below watched in stunned silence.

"Pho!" cried Thu, racing through the crowd to reach the girl who had just defeated Luis. Drew had already worked out that this was indeed the young woman he had already heard so much about. As she embraced her mother, Drew turned toward the runes. The fifteen shards were smeared with blood, courtesy of Lord Luis' unfortunate end.

Pho turned to him. "You must be Andrew Saran," she said.

Drew nodded. "It's nice to finally meet you, Pho," he replied.

Tenebrae and the young boy, as well as Geetie and Crysthan, came up beside them. The crowd below erupted into the cheer, while the Belrench soldiers looked confused and leaderless.

"Pho!" cried Josh, as the pair embraced. "You're okay!"

"So are you," said Pho happily. "Hax! You did it!"

"Glad to be of help," replied the young boy.

"This is my father, Geetie!" said Josh, eagerly introducing Pho to his father.

"My, my," said Geetie, a big smile on his face. "You *have* been busy, my boy!"

Crysthan chuckled beside Drew. "All has ended well it seems," he said.

Drew nodded, as Tenebrae handed him some of the runes. "There's still a few to pick up," she said. "Can't have them just lying around."

Drew laughed. "Definately not a good idea!"

He and Tenebrae began collecting the dropped runes as their friends celebrated around them.

Drew studied the Weather Runes closely. *Torrent* allowed the control of rain. *Rumble* controlled the sound of thunder. *Flame* controlled the sun's rays. *Breeze* controlled the wind. And *Bolt* would summon lightning, useful for striking enemies. He smiled. But a feeling of unease quickly took it away. He was unsure if he – Andrew Saran – would control these runes, or if Jer-d would.

Chapter Thirty-One

Happiness coursed through Pho at her newfound freedoms. She had returned to live with her parents in Phārā. Her father had apologised for trying to make her marry Luis, and had sworn to never again put status before his family's happiness. Ara and her husband had travelled with Chip for a farewell feast hosted in celebration of the defeat of Luis and Pho's safe return.

"To Andrew Saran!" called Chip, toasting his glass.

"Please, please!" said Drew. "The cheers should go to Pho! She was the one who found the Ocean Sapphire in the first place, *and* defeated Luis in the end!" He looked at her warmly. "If it was not for her, we would never have obtained the Weather Runes."

Pho smiled. "Actually, Hax was the one who found the sapphire in that cave."

She looked with affection at Hax and his mother Aberdare who had joined them for the celebrations. Then she looked at Josh, the Harlelish Protector sitting beside her. Pho felt sad at his impending departure. He would be leaving tomorrow to return to Harleland with Drew and the others.

"I'll miss you, Josh," she said.

Josh sighed. "Yeah, me too," he said. Then he smirked. "I'm sure a livewire like you will be more than okay."

"No sign of Irk and Murk?" Geetie asked beside them, looking at Crysthan.

The Herk Captain shook his head. "I searched and searched," he explained. "Those two grunts have fled somewhere to hide. I have a sneaking suspicion that they'll stir up some sort of trouble in Xudm again in the future, knowing those two."

Chip nodded and seemed to consider Crysthan's words. He did not say anything, but instead returned to his food.

Pho ate her chicken. Her father had helped cook it, and it smelled and tasted delicious. She was grateful that things had finally started to look up.

After dinner, the merry gathering settled into their sleeping quarters for the night. Pho was sharing her room with Ara and Tenebrae. In her room, Pho went through her shell collection. She smiled when she saw her favourite nautilus. She was glad to be back with it again, after fearing she would never see any of her shells again just a week ago when she ran away. She remembered her father's advice to open a market stall to sell them. Yes. That is what she would do.

"I like your shells!" complimented Tenebrae.

"Thanks!" Pho muttered.

Ara smirked. "So, you and Josh, huh?" she teased.

"Shut up!" said Pho. He was sweet, but they had only just met each other, and he was leaving tomorrow anyway – Pho knew it would be impossible.

The three girls sat around and talked for the rest of the night. Pho listened to stories from Tenebrae that told of happenings across the sea in Harleland. She went to bed that night with visions of travelling through forests, valleys and fighting fearsome enemies.

***

Pho stood next to Drew in the ruins of an old temple. She looked around, confused. Was she dreaming? It looked real enough, and when she waved her hand in front of her face, there was no sign that she was indeed sleeping. She turned to Drew.

"Why are we here?" she asked.

Drew smiled. "We both carried the runes," he explained. "I think Pogoda wants to talk to us."

Pogoda! thought Pho.

The weather spirit himself wanted to speak to her again! Sure enough, there he was, walking through the ruined temple towards them.

"Well done to you both," he said. "Thanks to you, the Ocean Sapphire is safely in the hands of its rightful owner, you Andrew Saran."

Drew nodded. "I swear to protect these new runes the same way I have protected the others." Then he looked in fear at the spirit. "Octavia!" he said urgently. "How is he?"

"He lives, but barely," Pogoda explained. "If you leave tomorrow as planned, you shall arrive to save him just in the nick of time."

Drew breathed a sigh of relief. "That is good news," he said.

"And now to you, Pho," said Pogoda, approaching her. "Your bravery has been unrivaled by anyone for a long time. Be very proud."

Pho sobbed, her emotions getting the better of her. "Thank you," she said. "But now I think I just wanna go back to living a normal life."

Pogoda nodded. "Of course," he said. "Already I have asked you to do too much. For that, I am sorry. But thanks to you, the world is saved from the tyranny of Emperor Occitanie. But more importantly – it has delayed *his* plans."

Drew stared at Pogoda darkly. "This figure you refer to – it was never Shârvous or Luis at all."

"I sense you have spoken to him, then," Pogoda said. "He has spoken to both of you, in voices and whispers. For he came for us you see, and now wields influence over both the Shadow and Weather Runes. Only Lazarka was able to hold out against him, while I am in a constant tussle for control over my own runes. Remember the last two lines of the prophecy–

But to end the dark, one must know,

Defeat the evil, and another will grow.

–the dark of Luis is defeated, but a new one – Jer-d – is growing stronger."

"That's why I've never spoken to Saran, then," said Drew. "Because Jer-d defeated him and took control of the Shadow Runes."

Pogoda nodded in confirmation. "You shall learn more in the coming months Drew," he said. "But for now, enjoy this victory."

He looked warmly at Pho, Drew doing the same.

"Thank you, Pho," Drew said.

"We shall never forget the help you gave us," said Pogoda. "The Demi-gods shall always shine favourably upon both you and your descendents."

With that, Pho woke up.

***

Chip had taken temporary command of Phārā while the Belrench regrouped. He had ordered for *The Ocean Herald* to be towed to the docks so that the Harlelish travellers could return home. Pho marvelled at the design and architecture of the ship. Josh had told her that even bigger ones existed moored in the Port of Boron Nigh on the other side of the mighty blue ocean.

"I shall return for trade!" Geetie called. "Xudm is rich in fresh ingredients – heck, I shall even compose a song in its honour!"

Tenebrae laughed. "Well, we have our on board entertainment sorted for the return journey," she said.

"Perhaps I can share a tune or two from the Crownlands," suggested Crysthan.

"It would be a pleasure, friend!" said Geetie happily.

Drew shook Pho's hand. "Farewell, Pho," he said. He turned to Tenebrae. "Ready?" he asked.

"Always," she replied.

Geetie came up to Pho and hugged her. "Good bye, dear Pho! When I return here we shall meet again!"

"Of course, Geetie!" she replied. "It will be a pleasure."

A tear fell down her face. Despite only knowing them a short amount of time, she would miss the Harlelish travellers.

"Oh, don't you start, or I'll start!" cried Geetie laughing, tears forming in his eyes. "Good luck, people of Xudm!"

"Farewell, Geetie!" cried Chip.

"Good bye, Pho," said Josh.

Pho smiled. "I'm glad we met, Josh," she said. "If your father visits here for trade, come with him and see us!"

"I will!" replied Josh. "I promise." He turned to Drew. "We still have one more set of runes to find."

Drew nodded. "Before we go…" he began. "Josh, you've been the best apprentice any Protector could ask for. And–" Drew ripped Josh's apprentice ribbon from his armour. "You're not an apprentice anymore. You're a full Protector of Harleland now. Your training is complete."

Josh smiled. "Thanks, Drew."

Tenebrae punched Josh playfully on the shoulder.

"Congrajulations, bud," she said.

Josh hugged her, before moving close to Pho, embracing her as Tenebrae turned toward the ship. Josh and Pho broke apart, and he joined Drew and others aboard *The Ocean Herald.*

"Bye, Pho!" called Tenebrae, while Crysthan also gave a salute of farewell.

"Drew, use those runes to clear the weather would you?" called Geetie.

Drew laughed, and he withdrew two of his new, sapphire runes.

Torrent. Breeze.

The wind slowed, and the rain clouds on the horizon dissipated. Pho sighed. They would have a safe and smooth journey home.

"Good luck!" called Josh as the vessel pulled away from the shores of Xudm.

Pho turned to Ara, Chip and Thu. "I love you guys," she said.

Chip smiled. "So do we, Pho," he said.

They sat in the light of the setting sun watching the waves, the mark that a new era in Xudm was about to begin.

About The Author

M.L. Hendry

Matthew Hendry first began writing stories as a child, slowly making them less embarrassing over time. In 2012, he began writing a story with help from his brother Jordan. Several years later, Matthew decided to use that tale as a basis for his first novel *Great Tower*, which he published in 2024.

Outside of writing, Matthew is a keen NRL fan (his beloved Canterbury Bulldogs might finally be on the up), and he enjoys travelling, having been to several European destinations with a strong desire to explore more.

Books In This Series

The Great Tower Saga

Andrew Saran is destined to master the mysterious runes, going on dangerous quests and meeting new and interesting people as he tries to save Harleland from Duke Shârvous… And perhaps other, darker threats…

Great Tower

In the Kingdom of Harleland, a young orphan is tasked with a dangerous quest to save his land from a destructive civil war.

Green Tree

As warring factions tear Harleland apart, Drew and a young Protector called Naz emerge as the last hopes.

Black Fortress (Coming Soon!)

As the influence of Jer-d grows, Drew, Josh and Tenebrae must find the last of the runes – before the final battle destroys not only Harleland, but the entire world.